STEP RIGHT UP

CARNIVAL OF MYSTERIES

L A WITT

Welcome

Traveler

Step Right Up

First edition

Cover Art by Dianne Thies, LyricalLines.net

Editor: Mackenzie Walton

Ebook ISBN: 978-1-64230-149-6

Paperback ISBN: 979-8-38793-475-9

Hardcover ISBN: 979-8-39083-381-0

❀ Created with Vellum

CONTENTS

CHAPTER 1

Jason

"*T*hat artist *sucks*." Mark pushed the drawing away on the weathered picnic table and testily yanked a fry from the massive pile we were all sharing. "It looks nothing like me."

Beside him and across from me, Ahmed seemed to be fighting hard against a frustrated sigh. I didn't blame him—his boyfriend was enough of a dick to begin with, and he'd only get worse if Ahmed dared to express distaste over anything.

Ugh. You deserve so much better. I took out my own frustration on a fry, jamming it into a paper cup of barbecue sauce. *Just dump his sorry ass already.*

"It looks fine, baby." Ahmed gestured at the piece of paper. "It's a caricature. They're *supposed* to be a little ridiculous."

Mark rolled his eyes and pointed in the same direction

with a fry, nearly splattering mustard on the picture. "I was *smiling*, and he made me look like… He made me look…"

"Like you're about to punch someone?" Lucas offered.

"Constipated?" his fiancée, Tina, suggested.

Mark shot them both a glare that matched his caricature perfectly. I had to bite back a laugh, which got a lot harder to do when Ahmed met my gaze across the table. He, too, was clearly trying to smother his amusement, since Mark wouldn't be happy if Ahmed laughed at him. Tina and Lucas didn't bother hiding theirs, though, and they snickered and fist-bumped.

In an attempt to calm Mark down so Ahmed's evening might not get any more miserable, I said, "The whole idea is they kind of exaggerate your features and then make you look ridiculous. He probably saw that you were happy and decided to make you look like that"—I tilted my drink toward the drawing—"to be ironic. That's all. I mean, look at how he drew Ahmed."

Ahmed craned his neck. "What's wrong with how he drew me?"

"Nothing. But this wasn't how you looked while he was drawing you." I gestured at it again.

Everyone peered at the caricature, focusing on Ahmed this time instead of cranky Mark. Then there were nods all around as they, I assumed, saw what I saw—a tired, subdued version of Ahmed despite him struggling not to laugh the entire time (mostly because of all the good-natured heckling we'd thrown his way). In the picture, he was smiling, but it was weak and forced, his down-turned eyes giving him away. It was actually heartbreaking to look at.

"So he made you guys like the opposite of what you really were," Lucas said. "Because you both look miserable even though you weren't while you were sitting, you know?" He turned to me. "What did he draw for you?"

I cringed inwardly because I wasn't fond of the piece I'd gotten from the artist either. Sheepishly, I showed it to them, which got more laughs from everyone. Understandable, since everyone here thought I was even crankier than Mark when it came to love and relationships, and the artist had drawn me with hearts in my eyes and floaty hearts around my head. Totally the opposite of reality.

I glanced at Ahmed, who was chuckling now, and...

No, the floaty hearts were the *opposite* of reality. Especially since getting this fluttery feeling over Ahmed just depressed me. Oh, yeah, I definitely had some feelings for him, but they were unrequited because he was out of my reach and very firmly with *that* guy.

Yeah. Heart-eyes, my ass.

"Jason makes a valid a point." Tina held up the caricature the artist had done of her. "I mean, the guy made me, of all people, look *drunk*."

He really had—her eyes were going in separate directions and her lips were quirked in a way that suggested she was slurring her speech or something. She was nearly tumbling off the seat, too. It was a hilarious picture, especially considering she never, *ever* drank alcohol.

To my great relief, the comparison to her wildly inaccurate caricature seemed to work. Mark eyed the drawing, then shrugged and lost some of the tension in his shoulders. "I guess? I don't know." He tugged another fry from the pile and added a sullen, if less hostile, "I don't like it."

He was annoying and pathetic when he was pouting, but that was far easier to put up with than when he was pissed off and ranting and raving. Especially since Ahmed could just quietly roll his eyes or suppress chuckles rather than walking on eggshells.

I, however, was still pissed off. That had quickly become my default state whenever Mark was around, but I'd learned to keep my irritation out of sight. I'd dare say I'd developed an almost superhuman ability to put on a smile and not let the asshole catch on that it wouldn't have hurt my feelings if the mayonnaise he was dipping his fries into had gone unrefrigerated for too long.

Okay, I didn't actually want him to die or anything, but he sucked, and I wasn't a saint, and yes, there were moments when I wished he had to spend an entire outing in the restroom. Was it really too much to ask for him to lock his miserable self in an overheated Porta-John for a few hours while the rest of us had fun?

Yeah, probably. But I didn't feel too bad about it, considering how he treated Ahmed. And given the choice, I'd have greatly preferred to never spend any time in his prickly company. What could I say? I fucking hated the guy.

But I *really* liked Ahmed, and Mark didn't like Ahmed going anywhere without him. When our coworkers wanted to go out, which we often did, it was either Ahmed came with Mark or he didn't come at all. Given the choice, I always preferred to have him there. Mark was, unfortunately, the price of admission.

As everyone continued eating and chatting, I surreptitiously watched the couple across the picnic table, I wished for the millionth time that Ahmed would just dump his ass. What did he even see in him? Was it just inertia? They'd been together so long, it didn't even cross Ahmed's mind that he might want—not to mention deserve—something better? Because Mark had been insufferable every time we'd ever met. There hadn't even been that honeymoon period where you meet a new person and they're on their best behavior for a little while before they start showing their ass. No, from the moment I'd met him, Mark had been obnoxious, bitchy, and inescapable. The human equivalent of tinnitus.

Oblivious to me, Ahmed laughed at something, and my

heart did things it shouldn't have done over someone else's boyfriend. The carnival was lit by hundreds of those big incandescent bulbs in a million different colors, and Ahmed's smile made the whole place ten times brighter. And that was while he was still reserved and restrained by his boyfriend's presence; if he gave one of those relaxed, easy smiles I saw so often at the clinic when Mark wasn't around, the brilliance would probably blind everyone here.

God, Ahmed. You deserve to smile like that all the time.

Sometimes I wondered if I was just being selfish. I was admittedly jealous of Mark. I'd had the worst crush on Ahmed since the day he'd started at our clinic, and that hadn't abated in the slightest in the three years we'd been working together. He was so sweet, and funny, and…everything.

And yes, he was hot, too. That was what had caught my eye the first day, of course—it was impossible not to notice such a beautiful man. He'd mentioned at some point that his dad was Iranian and his mom was Syrian, and he had a photo of them on his desk. He had his dad's stunning dark eyes and high cheekbones. His mischievous grin had clearly come from his mother, and he also had her kind smile. Sometimes he let his beard get a little rough and scruffy. Other times, like now, it was short and meticulously trimmed, emphasizing his sharp jawline.

He was just…

Christ, he was beautiful. Especially when he could laugh and joke freely instead of holding back like he always did around Mark.

And the thing was, the physical attraction had only ignited the crush. It wasn't what had me losing sleep and forgetting how to do my job now, three years later.

Yes, he was pretty.

Yes, he was adorable.

But he was also one of the sweetest, most kindhearted people I'd ever known. We worked together in a family medical clinic, and everyone from the doctors on down knew that if a child needed comforting, Ahmed was the nurse to send in. He could talk any child through a shot or soothe the unhappiest crying baby. Every patient raved about how he listened, took them seriously, and didn't dismiss or patronize them.

Watching him in action melted my heart every damn time.

In fact, I was pretty sure I remembered the exact moment when my lingering crush had rocketed straight to falling in love with him.

"I know it hurts," he softly told a little boy with a painful sprain who'd been struggling so, *so* hard against the tears that wanted to fall. *"It hurts, and you're allowed to cry if it hurts. It's okay. Let the grownups be brave and take care of you.* You *don't* have *to be brave."*

Immediately, the boy had broken down crying, and his mom followed Ahmed's lead—comforting him, but not trying to make him think there was anything wrong with crying. So many parents praised their kids for being brave because they didn't cry, but Ahmed always told them, kindly and gently, that sometimes it was okay to not be brave. And more often than not, the kids who took him at his word seemed to relax. As if trying to deal with the pain and fear *and* be brave took a huge toll, but once they let the dam break, it knocked a ton of weight off their poor tiny shoulders.

Small wonder he was the most popular nurse at the clinic, and not one of us was salty about it.

His boyfriend, however…

I slid my gaze to Mark, then rolled my eyes and went for my drink. I was here to have a good time tonight, not wallow in much I couldn't stand that jackwagon. So, I just shook away my thoughts and amused myself by thinking about how sad I wouldn't be if a ride operator failed to properly secure Mark's safety harness. Probably not a recipe for good karma to have those thoughts, but he was being a dick to the man of my dreams, so…meh.

"Oh, hey." Tina started thumbing something into her phone. "Derek just texted—said they're parking now, and then they'll be on their way in."

"Sweet!" Ahmed lit up again. "Did they say which entrance?"

Tina furrowed her brow at the screen. Then, "The one we came in. I'll just have them meet us here, since they'll probably want to eat."

Mark huffed and rolled his eyes. "So we get to sit here for *another* hour instead of…" He gestured around the carnival.

Ahmed indulged in an eyeroll too but quickly schooled his expression. "We could go walk around." He motioned toward me. "You, me, and Jason. Then after everyone else eats, we can all meet up again."

Mark and I locked eyes across the table, and he looked about as thrilled at the idea as I was. He was probably reconsidering, thinking that staying here at the table wasn't so bad after all, but I was in the mood to antagonize him, and I beat him to the punch.

"Great idea!" I rose and started to collect my things off the table. To Tina, I said, "Why don't you guys meet us at the carousel? It looks pretty central."

"Sounds good!" she chirped with an extra bright smile. She made a face at Mark's back, which didn't surprise me; she was probably thrilled to be away from him for a while.

I, however, was not getting such a break, probably because unlike Tina, I'd always managed to keep my distaste for Mark out of Ahmed's sight. Which explained why he'd thought nothing of inviting me along while Lucas and Tina went to meet the rest of our friends.

When Tina's eyes met mine, I mouthed, *"You owe me."*

She just giggled.

We finished gathering our stuff. Both Mark and Ahmed's caricature and mine went into Ahmed's backpack, and after we'd tossed our trash, we picked up our drinks and started walking. I made sure my phone was on vibrate so I wouldn't miss when Tina texted. While we wandered, she and Lucas would meet up with Connor, Derek, Isaac, and Peyton. Derek and Peyton worked in the radiology clinic above the family practice where I worked with Ahmed and Lucas. They were bringing Peyton's roommate, Connor, as well as Isaac, who worked in the lab our clinic used. The plan had been for all of us to arrive at the same time, but a forgotten wallet and some traffic had waylaid them by an hour and a half. Good thing it was a Friday night and if this carnival was anything like the county fair, it would go until well into the wee hours.

While Lucas and Tina met up with the stragglers, Mark, Ahmed, and I wandered the long row of carnival games. None of us was in any condition to get on any rides—that could wait until our food had settled—but if there was one thing we could all agree on, it was that carnival games were a blast. So, why the hell not?

I had to say—this was an odd carnival, that was for sure, and not just because it was inexplicably in the middle of a field a solid hour away from town. Tina had found out about it via a flyer nailed—actually nailed—to a utility pole, and there wasn't a website to be found. The flyer was on thick paper with pictures of old-timey tents, wooden rides, and a fortune teller. We'd all figured that was just the aesthetic of their ads.

Nope—everyone and everything here looked like something out of a carnival or a circus that our great-grandparents might've gone to. There was one of those antique carousels, and it fit right into the look of the whole place. White paint and fabric had yellowed with time. Brass and leather were in good condition, but had enough tarnish and wear to suggest they'd been in use for many, many years. Instead of LEDs, the colorful lightbulbs glittering in every direction were old-school incandescent bulbs with those wire filaments that left white-hot after images if you looked at them too long.

Ride and game operators accepted paper tickets. No bracelets or smartphones or any of that nonsense. Actual paper tickets. Vendors took cash only, but who the hell carried cash anymore? Fortunately, the place was well-prepared for that—every time I heard someone ask where they could get cash, they'd be told there was an ATM "right over there." And there it would be. I never actually saw the machines while I was just looking or wandering around, even though they seemed like they should stick out like a sore thumb in this environment, but every time someone needed one, there it was—right over there.

The ATMs were the only modern thing in sight, but nothing seemed rundown or like it was about to fall apart. All the rides, booths, tents, and signs seemed sturdy and functional. In fact, the more I took in my surroundings, the more I thought it had all been built and painted to *look* vintage. People manufactured antiques and stuff, didn't they? Artificially aging them so they seemed older and could be sold for more?

Even that didn't quite fit, though. I couldn't put my finger on why, but I swore everything here really was as old as it looked…and yet it was all solid and in good enough repair that it might as well be brand new.

Apparently they really don't make things like they used to.

Despite the aged appearance, the carnival didn't have that

stale smell that reminded me of antique stores and grandparents' houses. The air was thick with buttered popcorn, rich chocolate, funnel cakes, and all those other flavors that screamed *carnival*. I was pretty good about watching what I ate, but if I made it through tonight without stuffing myself stupid, it would be a genuine miracle.

I'd already gotten a damn good start on that with the fries we'd all shared. Those had been heavenly. Like seriously, what kind of witchcraft was going on here that they could serve us an entire basket of curly fries—a gigantic brick that was the exact size and shape of the fry basket—and not *one* fry was over- or undercooked? Every single one, from those in the center to the bottom corners, was perfectly fried— crispy on the outside, soft on the inside. And every one of them, from the first to the last, was hot. Not enough to burn your fingers or tongue, but not lukewarm like the stragglers usually were. That didn't seem possible. And yet.

For that matter, as I walked with the guys from booth to booth and game to game, I didn't actually feel like I'd just gorged myself on fries. I was pretty sure I'd eaten more than I should've, but I just felt…good. Not hungry. Not like mistakes were made. In fact, I probably could've hopped on one of the more extreme flippy-downy-loopy-loop rides at the amusement park a few towns over without any issue, though I wasn't going to test that theory. Not even on the somewhat tamer rides rumbling and glittering around the edges of this carnival.

And did I smell corndogs?

Ooh, I might have to get a corndog. Or three. Should probably pace myself, but I could—

"Step right up!" a man at one of the carnival games barked. "Think you've got what it takes?" He made a grand gesture at the colorful game behind him. "Step right up and play for a prize!"

Ahmed peered at the game, then turned to us. "You guys want to?"

I scanned the booth. It wasn't a game I'd ever seen before. A hand-painted wooden sign declared that this was *Buttons of Mystery—A game for young and old!* Below that, *Find the secret —win a prize!*

Mmkay, then.

Beneath the sign was a row of three large wooden barrels that looked as old as anything else in this place. Each was filled to about two inches from the brim with buttons in every shape, size, and color imaginable. There had to be thousands in each barrel. Mother of pearl. Black. Blue. Red. Metal. Stone. Round. Square. Polygons. Rough. Smooth. Everything.

The guy running it was telling Mark and Ahmed the rules, but I swore this game was unlocking a core memory. Making me want to plunge my hands in and run them through the contents just like I had with that shortbread tin full of buttons that Grandma had always kept beside her sewing machine when I was a kid. I couldn't help flexing and straightening my fingers just imagining it.

Apparently the object was to feel around until you found something that wasn't a button. He wasn't more specific than that—just that you had sixty seconds to feel around, and when you found something that wasn't a button, you pulled it free, and the item you found would determine which shelf you could pick your prize from.

I was pretty sure I would normally start thinking there were gross or sharp things in among the buttons—and the healthcare provider in me did wonder about needles and broken glass, not to mention whatever microbes might be lurking in there. But despite my usual refusal to assume everyone around me had decent hygiene and that there weren't sharps or biohazards hiding like spiders in every

11

nook and cranny, I was mostly overcome with the need to *put my hands in the buttons.*

"What do you guys think?" Ahmed's eyebrows were up in that way that suggested he really wanted to do it, but he wanted to be sure we were also in. Probably because his papercut of a boyfriend would pout and complain if Ahmed wanted to play and he didn't.

Ugh, fuck that guy.

I cleared my throat. "Hell yeah, I'm in." I turned to Mark.

He frowned, because of course he did. "What would we even do with one of those?" He waved a hand at the prizes.

The question was…fair. The prizes weren't what I'd expect from a carnival, either. Not even this one. No stuffed animals ranging from pocket-sized to life-sized. No weird inflatable toys.

At first, I thought it was a bunch of postcards. On closer inspection, they were little wood panels, and the images appeared to be hand-painted just like the sign. Prints, of course, but they'd definitely been painted originally. The images were washed out and brownish like old photos, the colors faint as if they'd been colorized but had faded. I couldn't tell if they were colorized black-and-white photos of paintings, or if they'd been painted to look that way. They were styled much like the carnival itself—carousels, artsy closeups of lights or games or rides, some cotton candy. They were weird as hell, and… I kind of wanted one.

Almost as badly as I wanted to run my hands through those damn buttons.

We weren't the only ones who'd been drawn in, and we hung back to wait our turn. Some teenagers felt around, grimacing and giggling as they did while the man running the game kept time on an antique silver pocket watch attached to his vest by a chain. The rattle of the buttons gave me goose bumps, taking me back to afternoons at Grandma's house. Some nearby rides even added a rhythmic thrum that made me think of the familiar, comforting sound of her sewing machine.

Goddamn. I hadn't come here tonight to miss my grandma, but the memories this game was churning up were happy ones. Hopefully I wouldn't cry once my hands were in one of those barrels.

One of the boys suddenly yanked his hands free in a shower of buttons, a few of which scattered to the dirt at his feet, and he triumphantly held up…a golf ball. His friends whooped and cheered, and the man smiled as he let them choose from one of the shelves. The boy took a picture of an old tractor and tucked it into his backpack, and the kids moved on.

The next group was some teenage girls, and after them it would be our turn. The girls had been snickering the entire time, rolling their eyes and joking about the paintings.

"If I win one," the tallest of the group had declared, "It's going in the trash."

"Right?" another giggled. "Who the hell wants something like that on their wall?"

Despite their apparent distaste for the prizes, they ponied up the tickets and played. While they took their turn, the man kept time as he had before, but he also cut his eyes toward Ahmed. He looked him up and down. Then Mark. Then Ahmed again.

I watched, wondering what was going through his mind. Ahmed and Mark were clearly a couple, and Ahmed wasn't white. Either of those things could and sometimes did make people weird.

Don't be a dick, I mentally pleaded with the guy. *He's having a rough enough night being out in public with this jackass. Please, please don't be a dick to him.*

The girls finished emptyhanded, and they left,

complaining loudly about *"rigged games"* and *"I told you we didn't need an ugly painting anyway."* The guy with the pocket watch watched them go with a satisfied expression on his face before he shifted his attention to us.

"Welcome, welcome! Step right up!" He smiled broadly. "Would you like to win a prize?" He made a sweeping gesture at the barrels. "Five tickets a try!"

I almost whistled—at a dollar per ticket, that was not a cheap game.

Ahmed looked up at Mark, who still hadn't given a verdict. The man was looking expectantly at Mark, too, as if he thought Mark would be a gentleman and buy his boyfriend an attempt.

Pfft. That would be the day.

I made a decision instead and fished ten tickets out of my pocket. Nodding toward Ahmed, I told the guy, "Five for him. Five for me."

I was pretty sure Mark grumbled something. I was absolutely sure I didn't care.

Then Mark handed over five of his own tickets. The man smiled pleasantly and directed us to the barrels.

"Sixty seconds." He pulled out his pocket watch with a flourish. "Find the mystery!"

Ahmed and I exchanged grins and leaned over the barrels, hands hovering just above the buttons. We both laughed, because this was kind of ridiculous and silly. It was fun, too. It was a damn carnival—everything was supposed to be ridiculous and silly.

Beside Ahmed, Mark positioned himself as well, though he kept the sour look on his face. Whatever. If he was that determined not to enjoy himself, then that was on him.

"Ready!" The man gestured with his pocket watch. "Set! Go!"

We shoved our hands into the barrels, and instantly, I was transported back to those afternoons in Grandma's living room. The cool texture of the buttons between my fingers. The rattle as they moved inside the shortbread tin. Grandma's sewing machine. The radio in the background, playing songs from the 1970s while Grandma tsked about how she "felt old" now that the classic rock stations were playing the music she raised her kids to. It was all as vivid as if I were right there now, every button sliding between my fingers as familiar as the ones I'd played with thousands of times back then. I thought I could even smell that air freshener she always used, and was that a hint of the Tang she always made us drink with lunch? I'd hated that stuff, but it tasted like being at Grandma's house, and I suddenly wanted to find a glass of it so—

"Oh!" Ahmed yanked his hands free, sending buttons clattering everywhere, including a nickel-sized gray one that landed on the toe of my sneaker. In his left hand, he held up a metal spoon that looked like it had seen better days—bent, tarnished... but definitely not a button.

"Nice!" I said, still sifting through the buttons. Truth be told, I'd forgotten I was supposed to be looking for anything at all. In fact, I thought my fingertip might've grazed something not-button, but I was too focused on all the memories I was churning up to think much of it.

Our sixty seconds ended, and I slid my hands free. I felt... weird. Like I'd been someplace else, and for more than a minute. I didn't care if I'd won a prize or not. That moment in Grandma's sewing room was worth the five bucks and then some.

I shook myself as I realized Ahmed and the man were talking.

"Most people pick from *these* prizes." The man waved his hand at the wall of available pictures, but then he held up the spoon, and his eyes twinkled. "You found this, though. So that means you get one of the *special* prizes."

Mark snorted derisively. "Ooh, the spoon award. That's gotta be good."

The man shot Mark a look. By this point, Mark was scrolling disinterestedly on his phone, and Ahmed seemed to take advantage of his boyfriend's distraction to roll his eyes.

The man eyed Mark, his expression hard but otherwise difficult to read. Then his features softened, and he smiled warmly at Ahmed. "Wait right here."

As the man leaned down to get something from beneath the painted plywood table, Ahmed and I exchanged glances. We both shrugged.

My fingertips were still buzzing, my head still light, and I was seriously tempted to pony up another five tickets. Not for a prize—just another chance to run my hands though the barrel of buttons.

I suspected Mark didn't want to stick around, though, and once Ahmed had his prize, we'd likely move on. I could live with that. I'd just savor my newly sharpened memories and the lingering coolness of phantom buttons between my fingers.

"Here we are." The man rose, pulling out what looked like one of those drab green ammunition cannisters from one of the world wars. The latch shrieked in protest as he lifted it, and the top echoed that sentiment as it too was opened. From inside, he withdrew a stack of pictures not unlike the ones on the wall, though these were slightly larger.

On closer inspection, though, these *were* different. The images were more... I couldn't even put my finger on it. Just...more? The colors were still a bit muted, but more vibrant than the others. The images had more detail. More and deeper shadows. Instead of looking like forgettable post-cards, they were each striking in their own way, whether because of their unique compositions or their intense images. They even had little imperfections in the paint—a raised brushstroke here, a tiny crack there—that made me think these weren't prints, but actual paintings.

As Ahmed thumbed through them, I seriously considering taking another crack at the game in hopes I could win one myself.

"Ooh, I like this one." He tugged one free from the stack—an image of a carousel focused on three of the horses.

"What are you going to do with that?" Mark asked. "Do we need a merry-go-round painting in the house? Seriously?"

"I'll put it up at work." Ahmed smiled despite his boyfriend being a dick. "The kids will love it!"

"Of course they will," Mark muttered.

The man gave Mark a look. Then his eyes flicked to me, and he lifted his eyebrows as if to ask, *Is he for real?* That was when I realized that my earlier concern about him being weird over their same-sex interracial relationship had been way off base. No, he'd picked up on the *other* way their relationship was mixed—a really nice guy and an insufferable asshole.

I rolled my eyes and shrugged, hoping it conveyed, *Yeah, I know. What can you do?*

Shaking his head, he pursed his lips, but then his expression brightened again as he spoke to Ahmed. "The children will love it. Let me get you something to protect it."

"Perfect." Ahmed smiled back. "Thank you."

Mark sighed impatiently.

Because of course he did.

CHAPTER 2

Ahmed

I knew it was a mistake to come to the carnival.

The carnival itself wasn't the issue. It was weird and fun, and I could've spent hours—hell, days—exploring every nook and cranny of it. And it wasn't like this was one of those events that showed up annually like the county fair. No one had ever heard of this one, and God knew if or when it would come through again. We didn't even know how long it was in town—there were no dates on any of the flyers. It was just sort of…here. We'd all been too curious not to come.

And hanging out with my coworkers was always a good time. I worked with a great crew, all of whom were a godsend when we had micromanaging insurance companies and administrators and other bullshit to commiserate about. My job would've sucked without these people. And our patients. I liked our patients.

But anyway, I did enjoy hanging out with the group, and coming to the carnival with them had sounded like a blast.

The problem was Mark.

I loved him. We'd been together for five years. I lived with him, for God's sake, and we'd even talked about getting married.

But fuck my life, every time I brought him around my coworkers, my other friends, my family, whoever—it was a disaster.

And yet I kept doing it. Tonight, it was because I'd really wanted to come to this carnival, and if I didn't bring him, then I'd spend the whole evening feeling guilty for ditching him, not to mention dreading the inevitable fallout when I got home. Because there would absolutely be fallout. Especially if I had a good time *without* him and *with* them.

Jesus, this was exhausting.

As Mark and I wandered around with Jason while Lucas and Tina caught up with the rest of our friends, I was regretting my life's choices. Fuck. Mark could be pretty easygoing —okay, he wasn't, but when we were around my coworkers, he was insufferable. He spent the whole time in a constant state of clearly wishing he wasn't there, and he had an opinion about every-goddamned-thing.

"The county fair has way better rides."

"What the fuck is up with these garbage prizes?"

"A fortune teller? Seriously? Jesus fuck."

I gritted my teeth, fighting the urge to bite his head off. I'd had a long week. Was it really too much to ask to just *enjoy* some downtime?

Jason caught my eye, and he offered a sympathetic grimace, which he quickly schooled away when Mark looked his direction.

My cheeks heated. I hated that my friends had to put up with Mark. It was honestly a miracle they still invited me to anything, knowing he'd come along. They had to be sick of him by now, especially Jason, since Mark never seemed to miss an opportunity to take a swipe at him.

If you don't want to hang out with my friends, I wanted to tell him, *then stay the fuck home. Jesus.*

But if I said that, then he'd bitch because *I* didn't stay home, and I'd spend the whole time dreading the inevitable argument, and…

God, I was tired just thinking about it. Hopefully once everyone got here, we'd have a good enough time that it would make up for his attitude. Hey, maybe I'd even get lucky and he'd have a good time.

Yeah, I thought as I watched him sneering at the prizes offered by a ring toss game, *that'll be the day.*

Fortunately, Tina texted and said they were all heading to the carousel where we'd planned to meet, and we eventually made our way to meet them. Everyone took their sweet time getting there—stopping at shops and games along the way—but eventually, we met up with the group.

"Wow." Peyton gestured in the general direction of the entrance, brow furrowed. "I can't believe how far out in the middle of nowhere this place is. They couldn't use the fairgrounds?"

Tina shrugged. "Guess not? Maybe it was less expensive or something. Explains why everything is so cheap."

"Yeah," Mark groused, "except the tickets are a buck apiece *and* it's cash only. Who the fuck only takes cash in this day and age?"

"Who cares?" Connor said. "There's ATMs everywhere." He gestured past Mark. "There's one right over there."

I turned, and…yeah, there it was, between two game booths. Except I had literally just been standing there while Mark and Jason played one of the games. Like…*right* there.

But it wasn't like I noticed ATMs out in the wild on a regular basis, so it had probably just blended into the background like it would have in town or in a convenience store.

Right?

I shook myself. Whatever. It was there, and it just hadn't registered because I'd been busy watching my friend and boyfriend played Skee-Ball.

Now that everyone was together, we discussed what we wanted to do next. They had all eaten while they were waiting for us, but Isaac, Derek, and Connor all wanted to get refills of their sodas before we started walking.

While we waited for them, Peyton said, "So hey, on our way to get food, we checked out that place over there." They nodded past us and started rifling around in their bag. "The Plentiful Potions, or whatever it's called."

I glanced in that direction. Sure enough, there was a vendor's booth with a sign reading *Peter Parson's Plentiful Potions*. "So what'd you get? Shrooms?"

"I wish," Peyton grumbled. They held up a corked glass bottle. The bottle itself was cool—cobalt blue with some intricate designs on all four sides. "It's supposed to be a love potion." They chuckled and shrugged as a blush bloomed on their cheeks. "Couldn't hurt, right?"

"Hey, why not?" Jason laughed. "With the luck I've been having on dating apps, I'll try any damn thing."

"Right?" Peyton tugged at the cork, which was apparently stuck very firmly in the neck of the bottle. "Oh, come on." They grimaced as they pulled harder. "Is it supposed to work by making me go up to a random guy and ask him to open it like a pickle jar?"

Tina snorted. "I mean, if it works…"

"Seriously." Peyton pulled again. "What the fuck?"

Jason held out his hand. "Want me to give it a try? Because I'm suddenly invested in getting that thing open now."

Peyton laughed as they pressed the bottle into Jason's hand. "Or maybe you're just hopelessly in love with me and you want to use this as an excuse."

Jason rolled his eyes. "Uh-huh." He tried to twist the cork loose. "I think it would take more than a love potion to make me date you again."

Peyton feigned offense and mock-kicked his shin, but they both laughed, even as Jason grimaced and tried again to open the bottle.

I laughed, too, mostly to hide this weird flare of jealousy. Jason and Peyton had dated off and on before finally deciding they were better off as friends, though I was pretty sure they'd hooked up a time or two since then. And that was completely fucking *fine* because they were my *friends* and I had a *boyfriend*, and I was not at all *jealous* of—

"Oh, hey." I pulled my backpack down on my arm. "You guys have to see this thing I won playing a game."

"Yeah?" Peyton and Tina both perked up, expressions full of curiosity as they craned their necks.

"It's just some crap carnival trash," Mark said. "It'll probably fall apart in a week like anything else."

With my back safely to Mark, I made a face. Did he have to shit on everything? Seriously? I kept my voice even, though: "Maybe it will, but I think it's really cool. And it isn't like it cost me much—five tickets and less than a minute pawing around in a bunch of buttons."

"It cost *you* five tickets?" Jason guffawed as he continued with the stubborn cork. "Okay, Ahmed. Whatever you say."

I turned to him, meeting those playful hazel eyes, and my sour mood instantly evaporated. I laughed. "See? Even better! It didn't cost me a dime!"

Jason flipped me off. I snickered, then pulled out the painting, which the man at the game had carefully wrapped in purple velvet.

As I unwrapped it, Jason nodded toward it. "All joking aside, that thing is seriously cool, especially for a carnival prize." He twisted the cork again, to no avail. "I kind of want to go back and play again. See if I can win—goddamn, this thing will *not* move."

"For fuck's sake, numbnuts." Lucas gave an exasperated sigh, and he pulled his keys from his pocket as he reached for the bottle with his other hand. "Let's see you make fun of me for keeping a Swiss Army knife on my key ring now."

"Oh, I'll still make fun of you." Jason surrendered the bottle. "But this *one* time, I'll concede that it's useful."

"Uh-huh." Lucas flicked open the corkscrew and started on the bottle.

While he did that, I put the velvet aside and showed the painting to our other friends.

"Whoa." Tina gaped at it. "That is seriously cool. Is it…" She peered closer. "Wait, is that, like, real paint? Or a print?"

"I don't know." I shrugged. "Kind of looks real, but—"

"Of course it's a print," Mark said tersely. "There's no way they're giving away the real deal to someone who paid five bucks and pawed around in some buttons." He rolled his eyes. "They probably just textured it or something."

"It looks real to me." I ran my thumb along a brush stroke. "Feels real."

Jason leaned in, and he did the same, running his thumb along some of the texture. "Oh yeah, he's right. If this is a print or something, someone worked seriously hard to make it look like a real painting, because it's—"

"*Shit!*" Lucas yelped, and that was the only warning we had before a thick, syrupy liquid splattered on Jason, me, and the painting we were both holding. "Crap! I'm sorry! It suddenly came loose, and…" He made an apologetic gesture. "I'm sorry."

Jason and I looked at each other, then at the painting,

then at each other again. The goo was on our clothes and hands. We hadn't been completely slimed or anything—there were just viscous amber droplets all over the place.

I moved the painting to my other hand and shook out the one that had been splattered, not that it did any good. "Well...shit." I turned to Jason, and I realized some of it had hit him in the face. Mine, too, judging by the dampness on my cheek. I snickered. "Uh, guess we're lucky it isn't white?"

That got a snort out of Jason and a giggle from Tina. Even Lucas, who was still mortified, chuckled.

Mark, naturally, scowled.

Yeah, I was going to hear about that later. As if my crude sense of humor was anything new.

I tried to wipe some of the goo on my jeans. The carnival had left a thin layer of dust all over everything already, and I was going to do laundry tomorrow anyway, so what was a few sticky smears? Wiping it on my pants didn't do much, though. This stuff did *not* want to come off. It stuck to my skin *and* the denim, and now there were little pills of lint balling up in the smear on my hand. Fantastic.

"Jesus." Jason made a face as he tried to scrape it off on the edge of the picnic table, succeeding only in picking up a few chips of paint. "What *is* this stuff?"

"Eww." Tina wrinkled her nose. To Peyton, she said, "Maybe go ask the seller if they know how to get it off?"

Peyton nodded and jogged toward the little shop.

Lucas carefully took the painting from me, holding it gingerly to avoid getting the goop on himself. "I'm sorry, guys. I swear that cork was practically super-glued in, and then it just came flying off like it was pressurized." He shook his head. "I'm so sorry."

"Nah, don't worry about it." I wiped the back of my hand on Lucas's sleeve. "There we go."

"Hey!" Lucas stepped away, swiping at the sleeve. "Don't get—eww, oh my God. It's so sticky!"

"Yeah, it is!" Jason made a face. "Holy crap."

Someone retrieved some napkins from a nearby concession stand. They helped a little. Dipping them in a cup of water helped even more. The weirdly herbal-smelling wipes that came from the "potion" lady helped even more, and the goo finally released its hold on my skin and clothes. I didn't think I'd ever been so relieved to get a substance off my person, and I was a healthcare worker. Ugh.

"You want me to try to clean off the picture?" Tina asked.

"Could you?" I kept scrubbing at some stubborn residue. "I want to keep it, but—"

"Oh, Jesus." Mark rolled his eyes, his patience down to its last thread. "Just throw the damn thing away, or we're going to be here all night cleaning up."

"It's fine," I said as firmly as I dared when we were around other people. "It's almost—"

"Oh no!" Tina's head snapped up, and her eyes went huge. "I think it ruined your picture!"

"What?" I gently took it from her. Though she'd managed to dab away the splatters with the wipe, it was still plainly obvious where the liquid had landed: everywhere it had touched, the color was gone. The lines were still there, but the color was completely gone, as if the liquid had dissolved a layer that had been painted on top of a black-and-white image.

"That's so weird." I cautiously ran my fingers over the "holes" in the image. There was no difference in texture. I couldn't feel where the color ended. The tackiness was gone, too, which was a relief—I could live with the weird new look as long as it wasn't sticky.

"See?" Mark said. "I told you it was just cheap trash."

"It's fine!" With a shrug, I met Tina's gaze and smiled. "It's fine. Looks kind of cool, actually." I started wrapping it in the velvet again and pushed it into my backpack alongside the caricatures. "Now let's get moving so we can still enjoy the carnival."

I didn't miss the exasperated looks my friends were exchanging, complete with eyes flicking toward my boyfriend. Nor did I miss the way Mark swore under his breath.

But once the prize was tucked away and the wipes were tossed, we were all on the move again, hunting down rides, games, snacks, and whatever else this bizarre carnival had to offer.

And cranky boyfriend be damned, I was determined to have a good time.

DESPITE THE MINOR mishap with the "potion," our evening at the carnival was a lot of fun.

The same could not be said for the drive home.

"Are you fucking kidding me?" Mark shouted into his phone as he paced back and forth in the headlight beams on the grassy shoulder. "Three hours? It's one-thirty in the goddamned morning! What am I supposed to do?" He flailed his hand even though the roadside assistance operator couldn't possibly have seen him. "Just…sit here with my thumb up my ass until someone shows up?"

From where I sat on the guardrail a few feet away, I watched my furious boyfriend pacing and shouting and cursing into the phone. I silently prayed that the person on the other end didn't de-prioritize us just for spite and wait to dispatch a tow truck until daylight. I wouldn't have blamed them if they did—I'd been working with the public for far too long to criticize anyone for deliberately inconveniencing someone for being an asshole. I just really, really hoped they had mercy on Mark this time, if only so I didn't have to stay out here with him all night.

I pulled my gaze away from Mark and stared at the stretch of deserted highway we'd come down. We were somewhere in the broad expanse of farm country between the field where the carnival was set up and town. If I had to guess, we were about halfway home. All I could go by was how long we'd been driving, though; there were no landmarks out here. There wasn't a building in sight. Even if there were billboards or distinctive fences we could use to gauge where we were, we couldn't see shit. Everything was pitch black except for the pale glow from our headlights, the blinking amber of the hazards, and the twinkling red LED road flares we'd put down.

Good thing that new cell tower had gone up last summer, or we wouldn't have had any signal. As it was, Mark had been on hold with roadside assistance for ages before he'd finally gotten through.

All told, between the time we'd spent trying to figure out what the fuck had happened and how long Mark had been on hold, we'd been sitting here for a solid forty-five minutes. In that time, I hadn't seen a single other car go by in either direction. On a normal night, that wouldn't have been unusual—why the hell would anyone be out here at this hour?

But it had taken us a good fifteen minutes to get out of the carnival's parking lot. There'd been a mass exodus in progress, with taillights forming a glowing red centipede that twisted and wound for what seemed like miles. We'd hardly been bringing up the rear, either—there'd been plenty of cars behind us. And then... they were gone.

We hadn't gone the wrong way, had we?

Except there really wasn't a wrong way to go. The carnival was just off the highway, and between there and town, the only turnoffs were onto people's driveways, down dirt roads, or into that one ancient gas station with the old café. It was literally impossible to go the wrong way as long as you made the correct turn coming out of the carnival, and I knew for a fact we had. And there'd been cars in front of and behind us when Mark had hit whatever he'd hit— someone had even honked and swerved to avoid us.

But less than a minute later, as we'd stepped out of the car on the shoulder, there hadn't been another car in sight.

Where had they all gone?

I chafed my arms even though the night was still thick with the lingering heat of the summer afternoon. This was weird. Like, *cue jump scare in a horror movie* weird, and I was not a man who was easily spooked.

"You can't be serious!" Mark's voice echoed for miles. "It isn't like there's a damn blizzard and people are sliding into ditches!" He paused. Then he groaned and grumbled, "For fuck's sake. *Fine.*" Then he was speaking just loud enough for me to hear his irritation but not make out the words.

Great. We weren't going anywhere any time soon, were we?

But seriously, where the hell was everyone else?

Including our friends, now that I thought about it. Mark had been long past ready to call it a night, so we'd been first out of the gate while the rest of our group had lingered to say their goodbyes (and probably enjoy a few minutes without Mark). They would've had to pass us by eventually, right? I mean, maybe they hadn't recognized Mark's car. It was just a generic silver sedan, so it didn't exactly stand out in a crowd.

Still. Lucas drove Tina nuts by stopping just about any time he saw a car on the side of the road. He'd been an EMT before he'd gone to medical school, and first responder habits died hard. Peyton was a mechanic in their spare time and Connor was a paramedic, so same deal.

And Jason…he was absolutely wired the same way. His back had stopped him from becoming an EMT, so he'd gone into nursing instead—still strenuous on the body, but less so than working on an ambulance. Like Lucas, he wasn't one to drive past someone who might need help. Especially not in the dead of night. *Especially* not if it might be someone he knew.

So three carloads of friends with first responder instincts, all of them well behind us when we'd left the carnival, and they'd all gone right by us? Or vanished into the ether along with everyone else who'd been leaving around the same time?

I was confused and also a bit stir crazy, so I took out my phone and sent a group text to everyone who'd been at the carnival with us.

Car's fucked up. Waiting on roadside. Did you all make it home?

Instantly, multiple people were typing.

What? Where? Tina wrote. *Are you guys okay?*

Jesus, dude, Connor said. *Is that why no one replied to our texts? What happened?*

"Your texts?" I muttered into the air. "What texts?"

Do you guys need help? Jason asked. *We're at the trucker café. Can come help if you need us.*

Oh, so they were at the café by the old gas station. Explained why we hadn't seen them go past. But like, did that mean everyone from the carnival had stopped there? Because we hadn't seen *anyone*. In close to an *hour*.

I glanced at Mark, who was still pacing with the phone pressed to his ear. He raked a hand through his hair and swore.

To my friends, I wrote, *We're ok. Hit something. Mark thinks*

29

the front axle is broken. Car isn't drivable so we're waiting for roadside.

Do you need help? Jason asked again. *I can give you guys a lift home.*

I thought about it. From Mark's furious ranting and raving, the alternative was staying here for a few hours while we waited for a tow. If Jason took us home, we could get some sleep, then come back tomorrow and deal with the car.

"Hey, Mark?" I called out.

He spun on his heel and growled, "Hold on," to the person on the other end. "What?"

I held up my phone. "Everyone's at that café. Jason says he can pick us up if we want." Lowering my phone, I shrugged. "At least then we don't have to sit out here all night, you know?"

Mark scowled. He was quiet for a moment, then said to the person on the other end, "We'll get a ride and call someone who's actually helpful in the morning." And without waiting for a response, he ended the call.

Well, we were committed now. Mark would be salty for the rest of the night, but at least we'd be home instead of out here.

I texted Jason privately: *You don't mind? Tow truck told Mark it would be like 3 hours.*

In seconds, he responded: *I'm on my way. Send me your location?*

For a heartbeat, I was irrationally sure my phone wouldn't be able to find us. That we'd been transported into some weird parallel dimension while everyone else who'd been at the carnival drove down the highway like normal.

But my phone found us, and I sent the location to Jason.

I'd barely hit Send when headlights appeared in the distance. What the fuck? The café was at least five miles from here, and Jason would never drive that fast in an area with so many deer.

But then more headlights emerged from the darkness. And more. Still more.

Before long, there was a steady stream of vehicles passing us by, including a souped-up truck that I distinctly remembered from the carnival's parking lot.

"Oh. Sure." Mark gestured sharply at the flow of traffic as he sat down on the guardrail beside me. "*Now* everyone goes by." He tsked. "Maybe if your friends hadn't stopped to eat, we could've been home by now."

I bit back an aggravated sigh, because now was not the time for a fight. "Or *they* could all be home by now, and we could still be waiting for a tow."

Mark made an unhappy noise. Which, now that I thought about it, described most of the noises he'd made tonight. If he wasn't snorting derisively or muttering under his breath, he was complaining about everything from the caricaturist's work to what Peyton's "potion" had done to my shirt. He was probably even pissed off he hadn't been able to find a legitimate reason to bitch about the food, since that was one of his favorite ways to express his displeasure whenever we went out with my friends. It was usually an easy target, since anyone could find something wrong with any food if they were determined to criticize it. Maybe I was just tired and bitchy myself, but to my unusually vindictive delight, the carnival's food had been beyond reproach.

As we sat here waiting for Jason, I caught myself wondering again if I should've just gone to the carnival without Mark. I'd have spent the weekend getting an earful about it, and there probably would've been a cold shoulder in the forecast for the next few days, but it was kind of like going out partying in college—the hangover was worth it for the fun I'd had the night before.

What did it say about my relationship when I was comparing his attitude to my liver pitching a diva fit the morning after? That was probably something to think about after I'd had some sleep. Right now, I was running on fumes and irritated that my fun night out had been derailed like this, and Mark had been pissy for hours even before his car had shit the bed, so we were probably both on a hair trigger for a fight.

Yeah, best to just let it go until tomorrow.

Right. Because I'll magically grow a spine between now and tomorrow.

I shook that thought away. Definitely not something to think about right now. I didn't need to fight with Mark *or* have an emotional breakdown because I was so fucking frustrated with my life and the man who was sharing it with me.

Right then, not a moment too soon, a turn signal appeared in the long line of white headlights.

A second later, the vehicle broke away from the flow of traffic and nosed onto the shoulder, hazards coming on as it slowed down and approached where Mark and I were sitting. The other headlights illuminated the silhouette of a mid-sized pickup truck, and I knew without a doubt that it was a blue Ford Ranger with a bumper sticker that read, *Get a grip—it was only a lane change.*

And for the first time since we'd left the carnival, I breathed a sigh of relief.

Jason was here.

Now we could go home.

CHAPTER 3

Jason

I parked my truck on the shoulder, and I let relief wash over me.

I'd had no reason to expect Mark and Ahmed to not be here, but it was still a relief to see them. Yeah, even Mark. I didn't like the guy, but apart from some horror film fantasies, it wasn't like I wanted anything to actually happen to him.

Aside from getting unceremoniously dumped. That would be totally fine. Universe, make it so.

I chuckled to myself as I got out of the truck but schooled my expression before they could see or hear me. "Hey, what happened? You guys all right?"

"Yeah, we're good." Ahmed pushed himself up off the guardrail. "Hit something, and..." He gestured at the car.

I put on my phone's flashlight and peered around the front of the car. As soon as I saw the damage, I whistled. "Holy shit." I glanced at Mark, then gestured at the wheel, which was jutting out from under the fender at an alarming angle. The vehicular equivalent of a catastrophic fracture or dislocation. "What the fuck did you hit?"

He swore as he came closer. Crossing his arms, he glared down at it. "I have no idea. Pothole or something, maybe?" He glanced around, then shook his head. "It's too dark to go looking, but it felt like a big ass pothole or…I don't know, something. Like it was the pavement, not something sitting on top of it, you know?"

I nodded as he spoke. "Must've been a big pothole." The roads out here were in decent repair, at least as far as county roads went. Some potholes, yes. Some chunks of pavement that had washed away during some of the flooding last spring. But a hole big enough to break his damn axle—how had no other car hit it? Unless he'd been drifting off onto the shoulder or something, but there wasn't much of a paved shoulder out here; you had about six inches at most between the barely visible white line and weeds.

Mark, for all he was an insufferable jerk, was a pretty competent driver. He'd had a couple of drinks earlier, but he always—including tonight—scrupulously stopped consuming any alcohol two hours before he'd be driving. Not even a sip of wine or anything. So he wasn't intoxicated. He never, ever texted or talked on his phone while he drove, and he never went more than five miles over the speed limit, unlike his lead foot of a boyfriend.

He had apparently just been unlucky enough to hit something just right and just hard enough to break his axle.

You better be glad you didn't hit it hard enough to hurt Ahmed, dickstain.

Unaware of my thoughts, Ahmed hugged himself and gestured at the highway. "I swear we didn't see a single car go by after we stopped." He flailed a hand at the long line of taillights. "Now…there they are."

"There was an accident." I gestured over my shoulder with my thumb. "About half a mile past the café."

"An accident?" Ahmed whipped toward me, eyes wide in the low light. "Oh shit. How bad?"

"Eh, nobody got hurt, but there was an extended cab dually involved that wasn't drivable. It blocked the road completely, and they had to wait for a tow before they could move anything." I motioned back in that general direction. "Not exactly sure what the deal was, but they started turning people around to take the long way, and that was when we all stopped to eat. We just figured you guys were ahead of the wreck."

"And they finally got it cleared right before you came to pick us up?" Mark sounded skeptical, though he sounded skeptical of most things I said, because fuck him.

"I guess?" I shrugged. "When I left the café, I was going to take the long way and then circle back to get you guys, but traffic was moving by then, so…"

Mark grunted something that made me think he definitely thought my story was bullshit. Too bad for him, I didn't care about his opinions about…oh…anything.

Beside him, Ahmed blew out a breath. "Well, at least neither of us has to work tomorrow." He wiped a hand over his face. "We'll get in touch with a tow company, and I'll drive him out to the car."

I wanted to suggest having Mark hitch a ride with the tow truck, but that would probably cause a fight between them. Mark was already in a mood thanks to his car being fucked up; no point in giving him a reason to direct his ire at Ahmed.

For now, the best thing was just to get them safely home.

The guys gathered a few things out of the car, including the backpacks they'd had at the carnival. Then we piled into my truck.

This turned out to be one of those rare moments when I wished I'd bought an extended cab pickup. It was just me, so it didn't make sense to have extra seats, but when I was crammed into the front with Ahmed sitting between me and Mark?

Yeah, maybe that extended cab wasn't such a bad idea after all.

The ride was long and mostly silent. Mark was clearly pissed off at the situation, and he didn't like me, so for Ahmed's sake, I didn't say anything. And Ahmed... Well, he must've been wiped, because he fell asleep against Mark.

Mark was still awake, staring out the windshield and not speaking. I was tempted to ask if he minded me putting on some music or a book, but who was I kidding? Mark minded anything I did. Especially if Ahmed liked it. If I put on some music that Ahmed also liked, then Mark would be even more of a dick.

While I drove, I wondered if Ahmed had to tread as carefully around Mark as I did. I mean, Mark presumably *liked* Ahmed, which had to earn him some more tolerance than I got. Ahmed wouldn't stay with him if he had to walk on eggshells all the time like I did whenever Mark was in the same room, right?

Mark wasn't dating me, and he was about as fond of me as I was of him, so I could piss him off just by breathing. Early on, I'd entertained myself by subtly antagonizing him whenever we were all in the same room. After all, if he was going to be that pissed off over me having the audacity to exist, then I might as well have some fun with it. It didn't even take much—just casually bring up a band or a movie he didn't like, and watch him get his panties in a wad.

But that hadn't lasted long. I'd quickly learned that the more I irritated Mark, the more miserable Ahmed was going to be, especially after the get-together was over and it was just the two of them again. Once I'd figured that out, I'd tried to make as few waves as possible.

Sometimes I bowed out of hanging out with the group at all, especially if I knew things were tense between Mark and Ahmed. I loved my friends and the things we did together, and I hated that Mark had that much of an influence on my time, but...Ahmed. There was nothing I wouldn't do to make him happy, even if that meant coming up with a bullshit excuse not to go out with him and our friends after work.

I stole a glance at Mark and Ahmed. Ahmed would've been almost impossible to see, illuminated only by the pale ricocheted glow of my headlights, but Mark had taken out his phone. As he scrolled, the light traced hints of both of their profiles—Ahmed sleeping and Mark scowling.

I gritted my teeth and stayed focused on the road ahead. Was this my fault? I mean, not their car stranded on the side of the road, but the whole evening? It wasn't like Ahmed had been able to hide how exhausted he was, trying to put up with his boyfriend's crap *and* have a good time, all while still dragging from a long week at the clinic. He might've enjoyed moments tonight, but I doubted he'd look back fondly on this evening as a whole.

Chewing the inside of my cheek, I tapped a finger on the wheel. Should I have bailed tonight? Would Ahmed have enjoyed himself more if I hadn't been there?

I glanced at them again, and fury dissolved the guilt that had been trying to set up shop in my stomach.

Ahmed would've enjoyed himself a lot more if *Mark* hadn't been there.

Except he would've been dreading going home, because we all knew Mark would give him no end of shit for going someplace without him.

No, there was no hope of Ahmed enjoying an evening out as long as Mark was in the picture. Yes, it was worse if I was there, because Mark hated me, but Mark was the source of the misery, not me.

Glaring hard at the road, I wondered if the carnival would still be in town tomorrow.

Because that potions vendor *had* to have something that a crime lab wouldn't detect…

THOUGHTS OF MURDERING Mark with a carnival poison kept me entertained for the remainder of the quiet drive. No, I'd never actually *do* anything to him—things like prison time, losing my nursing license, and my mom eventually seeing me on an episode of *Forensic Files* were pretty solid deterrents, and despite some darkly amusing fantasies, I was not a violent person. But hey, whatever it took to get through that painfully silent drive without losing my mind.

As I was pulling into their apartment's parking lot, Mark said, "Hey. We're home."

"Hmm?" Ahmed sounded adorably sleepy. Beside me, he started to sit up. "Holy shit. Did I fall asleep?"

Mark said something that sounded like an annoyed affirmative.

I stole a glance just to take in the sight of a barely awake Ahmed. Then I concentrated on the road, and I parked beside Ahmed's car. In Mark's parking space. There was a guest spot like twenty feet away, but I knew it annoyed Mark when someone parked in his designated space, and I couldn't resist being just a *little* passive aggressive.

From his scowl as we all got out of the truck, it worked.

Eat a dick, Mark. Isn't like you're going to be parking here any time soon.

But then I looked at Ahmed again, and the satisfaction

died away. He was exhausted, and I'd probably just antagonized his boyfriend enough to make the rest of his night even more miserable.

Damn it. Sorry about that.

Mark muttered a thanks and headed for the building as I pulled Ahmed's backpack out from behind my seat.

Ahmed hung back, glancing over his shoulder after Mark before he hugged me gently. "Thank you again for doing this. You're a lifesaver."

I closed my eyes, stealing a second to savor this, just like I always did when he hugged me. It was all I was ever going to get with him, so I made sure to enjoy it. "You know you can call me any time you need help." I released him and met his eyes beneath the streetlights. "I'm just glad I was close by so I didn't have to keep you waiting."

Oh, man. Even when he was tired and stressed, his smile was just...everything.

"I'm glad we didn't have to drag you too far out of your way," he said softly.

I'd go anywhere for you, Ahmed.

Good thing I was well-practiced at keeping things like that safely in my head where they belonged.

"It all worked out," I said. "Anyway. I should—"

"Ahmed!" his jackass of a boyfriend barked from the door to the stairwell with *no* regard for their sleeping neighbors. "Are you coming in or not?"

Frustration washed over Ahmed's features, but he quickly schooled his expression before turning and saying, not quite as loudly, "Be right there."

Mark shot me one of those looks that said he wished I'd drop dead—*feeling's mutual, pal*—before he stomped back inside.

Ahmed closed his eyes and pushed out a breath through

his nose. Then he inhaled deeply and looked at me. "I should let you go. Thanks again for bringing us home."

"Don't mention it. Have a good night."

"You too. I'll see you Monday."

Why does Monday suddenly seem years away?

"See you Monday." I started toward the open driver door, but I didn't get far.

"Oh!" Ahmed started unzipping his backpack. "I almost forgot." He riffled around, then produced my caricature and handed it to me.

"Oh, right. Thanks." I smiled even though I would've been perfectly happy if that picture had never again seen the light of day. Still, I took it.

The soft, tired smile from Ahmed was worth it.

We finally went our separate ways this time. I started the truck again, stole one last look at Ahmed before he stepped into the apartment building, and left.

The drive from their apartment to mine took all of ten minutes, but those ten minutes seemed to stretch on for hours tonight. It wasn't even from hitting red lights or getting behind someone who was terrified to go the speed limit. In fact, this time of night, the lights were all green and the roads were mostly empty apart from a few people heading to one of the manufacturing plants for the early shift.

The drive still took the usual ten minutes or so. It just felt like forever.

I was probably tired. It was stupid late, after all, and though the evening had been fun, it had also been long, and it had been on the heels of a long week at work. I was probably just in that mode where I was so desperate to go to bed that every step I took toward blessed sleep felt like ten steps backward.

I don't know. The whole night had been weird. Why should now be any different?

I finally made it home, though. My roommates' cars were parked in front of the house and on the curb, along with Dan's girlfriend's car. They'd all probably long since turned in for the night, and she was a light sleeper, so I was extra careful to be quiet as I let myself in.

After I'd brushed my teeth, I headed for bed, but I paused. Then I picked up the picture Ahmed had been carrying around for me all evening—the caricature the artist had drawn of me. Had that really just been a handful of hours ago? Because it felt like years.

Lying back on my bed, I stared at the drawing more intently than I had when my friends had been around. I'd looked at it then, and we'd all made comments about it just like we had everyone else's, but I hadn't wanted to draw more attention to it than necessary. Mark's bitchiness had proved to be a blessing in that respect; once he'd started complaining about the picture of him and Ahmed, everyone pretty much forgot about mine.

Everyone except for me.

Of course, the caricaturist had exaggerated my features and proportions. It was a cartoon. Fine. I wasn't bothered by that.

No, what bothered me was the lovesick expression on my face.

Even with the heart-eyes, it wasn't just Disney jaw-on-the-floor lovesick. There was no mistaking what the artist had been going for. Despite the cartoonish style, the longing he'd drawn into my face was so fucking real it actually had my heart aching as I gazed at it now.

While Mark and Ahmed had been sitting for their carica-ture, Tina had giggled over mine and said she'd never thought of me like that. I'd had some boyfriends since I'd known her, and she'd been around for my on-again off-again thing with Peyton, but I hadn't had a serious relationship in a long time. None of them even suspected I had someone who I hadn't told them about. So, lovesick me was hilariously ironic to all our friends.

It was cute and comical, Lucas had pointed out, the way this artist seemed to draw all of us as the exact opposite of what we were.

Except…

Maybe he didn't.

Because while most of the drawings he'd done tonight had been wildly different from reality, three of them were a little too on the nose—mine, Mark's, and Ahmed's.

I supposed it was impossible to imagine Mark being anything other than a grumpy dickwad, so… fine. But what about me and Ahmed? Had the artist caught me looking at Ahmed and decided to draw what he saw in my eyes? Shit, was I that obvious about it? Because I tried like hell to be subtle, and my friends hadn't seemed to notice, but if this total stranger could see it…

Damn. I needed to work on my poker face.

And Ahmed…

God. Thinking about the caricature of Ahmed intensified the ache in my chest. I had no idea what had inspired the artist to draw him that way—what he'd seen to make him choose that expression—but I believed to my bones that what he'd drawn was what Ahmed tried to hide from all of us.

He was always cheerful and optimistic. The guy who had everyone in the office laughing, or who could make someone having a bad day feel better. That was just his way. Ahmed was synonymous with happy.

But once in a while, his eyes gave him away. Especially if

he didn't think anyone was looking, the mask would slip and the truth would come shining through.

Despite his happy front, Ahmed was *miserable*.

I suspected I knew why, too.

I had no idea what his relationship with Mark had been like in its early days. There must have been some kind of honeymoon phase or something, right? Some sort of spark to make Ahmed think, *yeah, this is where I want to be*? But by the time I'd met the two of them, any spark like that was—as far as I could see—dead and gone.

It wasn't my place to say anything, though, and Ahmed was clearly trying—and succeeding—to keep it out of people's sight.

Just…not out of *my* sight.

Or, evidently, the scarily intuitive caricaturist's.

Something about seeing Ahmed portrayed like that by a stranger hurt even more than seeing that side of him myself. As if it meant the façade was cracking. That Ahmed was so unhappy, he couldn't keep it hidden anymore.

I wanted to believe that meant he was getting close to saying, *"This is bullshit—I'm out of here."* I was just afraid he'd keep slowly spiraling deeper into misery, going through all the motions of building a life with Mark even though it was painfully obvious he didn't *want* that life. They'd even started making noise about getting married.

I closed my eyes and rubbed my forehead with the heel of my hand. I didn't know if I could get through a wedding between those two. Like yeah, I was envious as all hell and would give anything to be the one marrying Ahmed—or just being with him if he didn't actually want to get married, since some people didn't. But that wasn't what had my throat tightening at the mere thought of watching them say *I do.* If Ahmed did want to get married, then his wedding should be one of the happiest days of his life.

And fuck me, but I just did not see any way he would be happy going through those motions with Mark. Not with how Mark treated him.

I stared up at the ceiling and sighed.

You deserve so much better, Ahmed.

I can see it. That caricaturist can see it.

I sniffed sharply and wiped my eyes.

Why can't you see it?

CHAPTER 4

Ahmed

*I*n an ideal world, Mark and I would've slept in the morning after the carnival. We'd have had some coffee, maybe shared some tired laughs about what happened to the car, and then driven back out to meet the tow truck while we chatted over Egg McMuffins.

In an ideal world.

In reality, I managed maybe an hour or two of sleep, and when I finally gave up around eight, Mark was already out of bed. His side was cool, too, so he'd been up for a while.

I indulged in a moment to stare up at the ceiling and swear as I let dread sink in. Today was going to suck. Mark didn't handle stress *or* sleep deprivation well, and he was going to be extra delightful once he had to cough up his deductible to get his car fixed.

"I'd rather have a high deductible and pay low premiums," he'd told me ages ago. *"I'm not going to let them scam me out of that much money."*

I'd tried to argue. After all, I knew a thing or two about

insurance and deductibles, and I knew from experience that you got what you paid for. Or, well, that was the ideal outcome. At the very least, you didn't get *more* than what you paid for. Getting bare minimum insurance with a sky-high deductible just meant coughing up a fuckload of money when you were already stressed out—be it over a health crisis or car repairs—and then having to fight for every penny of coverage after that.

And while I was thinking about it...did his insurance even cover a broken axle?

I cringed inwardly. It probably didn't. If we'd been in an accident with another vehicle, that would be different, but Mark had hit something. Something we couldn't identify, which meant we couldn't claim the county or whatever was liable.

Didn't insurance cover damage like that if you hit a pothole? I'd have to check. But my gut told me that even if it did, the deductible would mean Mark paid for the entire thing out of pocket anyway.

Oh, he was gonna be so fucking *thrilled*.

I grabbed a shower and got dressed. At first I was going to skip trimming my beard. I usually did that on weekends anyway, and if Mark thought I was dragging my feet and keeping him from getting his car taken care of, then he'd be a delight. But... he'd be a delight anyway, so fuck it. He could wait a few goddamned minutes.

When I made it out to the living room, beard freshly and meticulously trimmed, Mark was ready to go, which meant he'd expect me to follow suit. Given his scowl, I'd probably pushed my luck enough by taking so long to groom myself. If I knew what was good for me, I'd put my coffee into a travel mug.

Maybe it wasn't the most mature thing in the world, but I did take a few seconds to debate my options there before I decided I really didn't want to provoke him. Travel mug, it was.

As I took one out of the cabinet, Mark grumbled, "Hopefully the car isn't stuck in the damn mud now."

"The mud? Why would—" But then I glanced out the living room window, and I understood his comment: It was absolutely *dumping* down rain. We never got much rain in the summer. Enough to keep the farms watered (usually), but not...*this*.

Apparently we were getting it today, though. Holy crap.

I glanced at my scowling boyfriend, genuinely surprised I didn't see literal dark clouds swirling around his head as he fumed over the car, the weather, probably something or another I'd done, and God knew what else.

Well, wouldn't *this* day be fun?

I sighed as I started pouring my coffee but didn't say anything. Definitely not a good idea to provoke him more than I already had.

The thing was, I didn't have to walk on eggshells with Mark most of the time. Well, not much. He was incredibly particular about things being immaculately clean, about being early to everything, and about anything that wasn't done according to his exact specifications. I was used to that, and I was easygoing enough to just go with the flow. Most of the time.

He actually *could* be mellow and easygoing too. He could even be fun, though that seemed kind of novel these days, which probably should've been a red flag.

What are we doing? Do we even like each other anymore?

But that was stress and sleep deprivation talking. It had to be. I'd put a pin in it for now, and after the car was fixed and everything had quieted down again, I could revisit our relationship. Now was definitely not the time.

Neither of us said much on the way out to where we'd left

his car last night. Mark was stewing, which I expected. Me, I was half walking on eggshells, and half trying to concentrate on navigating with trash visibility. The rain was coming down so hard, it was like trying to drive through a damn blizzard.

When we made it to the car, which was on the opposite side of the highway, I put on my hazards and slowed to a stop. There weren't a lot of cars out right now, so it didn't take long for a break in traffic, and when it came, I made a U-turn, then pulled up behind Mark's car.

As I shut off the engine, I asked, "Any ETA for the tow truck?"

"Yeah, they said—wait, I just got another message." Mark paused. Then he huffed sharply. "Oh for fuck's sake. They're running behind." He threw open the passenger door, and as he got out of the car into the deafening rainstorm, he shouted over his shoulder, "They're estimating two hours."

I bit back a curse and let my head fall against the headrest as rain beat like hailstones on the roof and windshield. Seriously? Two hours? What were we supposed to do now? Just…sit out here until they showed up?

Not much else we could do, I supposed. Maybe go grab a bite to eat at the café, but that place could be really slow on the weekends, and if we missed the tow truck, then the day would just get shittier.

An incredibly tired and threadbare side of me wanted to leave Mark here to wait for the tow while I went home and continued about my day. I wanted to go to the gym. I had some laundry to catch up on. I needed some actual downtime to unwind from my job. Maybe take a nap in an effort to make a dent in last night's sleep debt.

But I wouldn't do that. Not to him. Not to anyone. No matter how frustrated I was with him and the world and every goddamned thing right then.

Stress and sleep deprivation. That was all it was. Tomorrow, we'd both be fine.

For now…

Well, there was nothing to do but wait for the damn tow.

There was no point in waiting for it out in the rain, though.

I sighed and stepped out of the car. "Hey," I called to him over the noise. "Let's wait in here. At least we'll be dry."

Mark was striding back toward me from his car, but he shook his head and gestured up the highway. "I'm going to go see if I can find what I hit." Without waiting for a response, he jogged past me, sneakers splashing in the water streaming along the weathered asphalt.

I watched him go, but it wasn't like I could argue with him. Even if he'd be willing to listen to reason right now — which I suspected he wouldn't—he wouldn't be able to hear me.

So, I got back in the car, already drenched to the skin. A second later, my phone chirped. I grabbed it, thinking Mark might've needed help or something. But the message hadn't come from him.

Hey, Jason had written. *Do you guys need help with the car? Since the weather went to shit?*

I glanced up at Mark's injured car, which was blurry through the water sliding down my windshield. Then I wrote, *Nah, we're just waiting for the tow. Not much to be done except wait.*

How is that going?

From anyone else, I'd think they were asking if we were getting bored and stir crazy. But Jason had never been great at hiding his reactions to Mark, and Mark was always extra pissy when Jason was around, so Jason had a lot of opportunities to roll his eyes or glare at my boyfriend's back or shoot me *are you okay?* glances when Mark couldn't see him. He'd ask me sometimes at work if everything was all right, and he always seemed genuinely concerned—even hurt—over tension between me and Mark.

So assuming I wasn't just imagining things, I could read between the lines of his question: *Is everything going okay with him?*

In my mind's eye, I could see him with his phone in one hand, car keys in the other, ready to sprint for the parking lot and drive like a madman into the storm if I so much as hinted that tensions were high out here. He probably wasn't, but picturing it gave me a warm feeling that I didn't want to think too much about.

We're fine, I told him. *Just dying of boredom, lol.*

Ok. Just hit me up if you need something.

Then he sent me a couple of memes from a nursing humor page we both followed, and I snickered as I laugh-reacted to them. I was about to hunt one down to return the favor, but the passenger door swung open and Mark dropped into the seat, sopping wet and mad as hell.

"Holy shit." He shook out his hands, sending droplets splattering all over the car and me. "What is up with this weather?"

I subtly slid my phone into the cupholder. "Did you find anything?"

Mark wiped rainwater off his face, plastering his hair to his forehead in the process. "Not a damn thing. Looks like the county came through and fixed a bunch of potholes and shit recently—the road is smooth as glass out there."

"Really?" I looked outside as if I could see anything through the sheets of rain coming down. "What the hell did we hit, then?"

"How the fuck should I know?" he snapped.

I drew back and put up my hands. "Hey, I'm just trying to figure out—"

"Yeah, well, I can't find anything out there, so you're sure as shit not going to magically have the answers sitting in here."

I pressed my lips together. Fine. No point in speculating out loud, then. He'd clearly reached the level of pissed where he'd bite my head off no matter what I said, so... I didn't say anything.

Long silence stretched out between us. I stared out the windshield because I knew if I took out my phone, that would be another landmine even though *he* was scrolling through *his*.

Were we always like this? Because I was pretty sure we weren't, but in that moment, it felt like we were. Like this was our default state. Or how we were more often than not these days.

That couldn't be right. Could it? No. I was just frustrated, and it was like how I'd explained an injury to a frustrated patient recently.

"It really will get better," I'd told them. *"In the moment, it always feels like you're never going to feel normal again and that you can't even remember what normal felt like. But this isn't a permanent injury. Give it another week or two, and it'll feel a lot better. In a few months, you'll probably be back to normal."*

Was that where I was with Mark? We were a few hours into a miserable weekend, and I was so exhausted and aggravated that I'd convinced myself this was my new normal? Or that it had been our normal for so long I couldn't remember ever being happy with Mark?

Maybe. Something like that. Unfortunately, my job also meant sometimes seeing people whose injuries or illnesses *were* permanent. Where they were sick or in pain, and that was their new normal.

But this isn't an injury or an illness. It's a relationship. I'm supposed to love him.

He's supposed to love me.

I stole a cautious glance at Mark, who was glaring at his phone.

I'm pretty sure he used to love me. Why can't I remember what that felt like?

I shook that thought away and stared at his rain-blurred car in front of me. Now really wasn't the time to be thinking about our relationship. If the roles were reversed and I was the one soaking wet and looking down the barrel of some expensive car repairs after a mostly sleepless night, I probably wouldn't be so great to live with either. How would I feel if Mark decided that was the moment to start telling me what an awful boyfriend I was?

And why was I so sure that was exactly what he would do?

Mark's phone pinged. A second later, he sighed with palpable annoyance. "Great. They're delayed again."

Oh joy. "How long?"

"At least another half hour on top of the original ETA." He put his phone facedown on his leg, jammed his elbow up against the window, and rubbed the back of his neck as he pushed out an irritated sigh. "What a shitty way to cap off a shitty evening."

My temper flared hot in my chest, but I tried my level best not to let it show. Still, I couldn't quite resist: "I thought you had a good time last night. I mean, aside from…" I nodded toward his car.

Mark laughed humorlessly. "Yeah. Okay."

I chewed on that for a moment. Let it go? Let it go. Except…fuck it. I wasn't having the greatest day of my life either, and I wasn't going to just sit quietly while he bitched. "What was wrong with it? The carnival was fun. The food was amazing. And some of the games were—"

"I don't like hanging out with your friends, Ahmed," he snapped. "They're annoying as hell."

"Why did you come with us, then?" Shit. So much for keeping my temper in check. "If you didn't want to go, then why—"

"What was I supposed to do? Huh?" He twisted in the seat so he was facing me fully. "Just stay home with my dick in my hand while you went out and had a good time?"

I threw up my hand and let it fall on the steering wheel. "You go out with your friends all the time! You're just as capable of doing something on your own as I am. Or you could've gone out with them last night while I was at the carnival!" I paused, and when I spoke again, I injected some calm into my voice. "We don't have to do everything together. If you don't enjoy hanging out with my friends, then it's totally fine with me if you want to do something else."

The sarcastic laugh set my teeth on edge. "Yeah, you'd fucking love that, wouldn't you?"

I narrowed my eyes. "What's that supposed to mean?"

"You know exactly what it means."

"No, actually I don't." I mirrored him, twisting as much as the wheel allowed. "What does it mean?"

Mark glared at me for a long moment, his expression telegraphing that he didn't buy that I wasn't tracking. When he'd apparently decided I wasn't bullshitting, he snorted and shook his head. "Oh, come on. What's not to love about hanging out with a hot coworker who's got chronic puppy dog eyes for you?"

I stared at him. "What are you talking about?"

"You don't see it?" He waved a hand. "Bullshit. It isn't enough to have him fawning all over you at work? You need to get your fix after hours, too." He glared hard at me. "And you'd just love it if I wasn't there so you could—"

"Mark. Seriously." I showed my palms. "I have no idea what you're talking about. These are my *friends*. That's it. I'm with you, not—"

"And if you had half a chance to put your dick in Jason's mouth, you'd do it. Don't fucking lie."

I was speechless, watching this man I'd actually been considering marrying. Where was this coming from? Even when he was stressed out and sleep-deprived enough to light into me about something, he wasn't usually *this* aggressive about it. He sure as shit never accused me of cheating or wanting to cheat, especially since infidelity was a red line for both of us. Plenty of our friends had open relationships or brought extras into their bed, and that was fine, but Mark and I both preferred monogamy. It was what we'd committed to from the start, making it clear that cheating was a dealbreaker.

And it was Mark, not me, who'd observed more than once that Jason was attractive. He was the one to snidely remark that Jason didn't have to wear shirts that snug when his arms and shoulders were that built, and did he always have to show off his tattoo sleeve? Or Mark would comment that it was a crime that gorgeous, hazel eyes like that were wasted on him. Or, when Jason had briefly dated a man who could have easily been an underwear model, that "blonds really do have all the fun."

He'd noticed Jason's physical attractiveness so much and so loudly that I'd have worried he might sleep with Jason if not for the fact that Jason clearly—despite his best efforts to hide it—disliked Mark.

Now *Mark* was accusing *me* of wanting to fool around with Jason?

"Do you…" I cleared my throat, then tried again. "Do you think I'm cheating on you?"

"Maybe not yet." He locked eyes with me. "But we both know it's only a matter of time."

"No, the fuck, it isn't! Jesus, Mark! Jason is my *friend*. Full stop. You're my boyfriend. Full—"

"Yeah, well." Venom dripped off every word. "Maybe I shouldn't be anymore."

My heart dropped and my spine straightened. "Are...are you breaking up with me?"

"Why not?" He shrugged sharply. "I'd rather nip this in the bud than wait around to catch you two in the act."

I didn't know if I was more hurt or angry, but I knew without a doubt that I was done with this conversation. "You know what?" I gestured at his car, then jabbed the button to start my own car's ignition. "Why don't you wait in there for the tow? I'll meet you at home."

He raised his eyebrows as if to ask if I was for real. The engine idled, the sound almost muffled by the roar of the rainfall. Since he apparently thought I was kidding, I shifted into Drive and released the E-brake. Then I watched him expectantly.

The standoff lasted for a few more tense moments before Mark shoved the door open and got out. The rain swallowed whatever he muttered over his shoulder. Fine. I'd heard enough from him for right now.

I waited until he was safely in his car, then peeled away and took off for home.

What the fuck?

What the actual fuck?

Where had this even come from?

And...what did it mean that, as soon as I was out of Mark's sight, my first impulse was to pull over and call Jason? Or to go to his place instead of home?

It meant he was my friend, goddammit. Mark was seeing

something that wasn't there, and if I went to Jason's place, it wouldn't be so I could dive into his bed. It would be because Jason would let me vent, and listen to me, and offer feedback if I asked for it, and probably calm me down enough that I could be objective about things. An hour or two with him, and I'd probably see things in a rational light that I couldn't right now. Hell, he'd probably have me laughing again, not riding this line between wanting to cry and wanting to throw something.

No, I couldn't go to Jason. Not for this. Not when he was the unknowing catalyst for some of it. Something about my friendship with Jason was bothering Mark, and if I had any hope of resolving things, I couldn't twist that knife. Especially not right now.

So I didn't pull over. I didn't call Jason. I just continued driving home.

All the way there, I vacillated between hope and *fuck this.* One minute, I hoped the time gave us both a chance to cool off and calm down, and a few hours from now, we'd be catching our breath after some makeup sex, and everything would be fine.

The next, he could go fuck himself, and I was mentally calculating how many boxes I should pick up so he could pack his things and get the hell out. Yeah, it was a shared apartment, but if he wanted to initiate the breakup, then *he* could go find a place to stay while I rode out the lease. Wasn't like he could pay the rent on his own anyway. I could.

Which was another point of conflict between us—he hated that I made more than him, and he never missed an opportunity to slap me in the face with it. It was probably an especially raw nerve right now as he faced down the cost to repair his car.

So maybe I shouldn't kick him out. Maybe I should go to my brother's place, and I could keep paying rent while I was—

No. Fuck that. If Mark wanted to leave, he could leave. I shouldn't have to shoulder the burden just because it would be harder for him to get on his feet. I'd try to resolve this and smooth things over, but if he really did want to end our relationship, then he could go through the motions.

Did he want to end it, though? For real? Or was he just pissed off and lashing out? It wasn't like him to throw down the breakup gauntlet, but when Mark lost his temper, anything was possible.

I had no idea what was happening. Or what was going to happen.

Right now, all I could do was wait for him to come home and go from there.

And I didn't know what outcome I was hoping for.

IT WAS a few hours before Mark came home.

By that point, I'd settled in to binge one of the shows he didn't like. The only time I could watch it was when he wasn't around, and I'd had nothing else to do, so why not?

But as soon as I heard his key in the door, I shut off the TV. My heart was in my throat as I turned around and waited for him to come in.

When he did, he didn't say a word. He didn't even look at me.

Instead, he took off his jacket and shoes, then stalked down the hall toward the bedroom. A drawer opened roughly. Then the closet door squeaked.

I swallowed. Steeling myself, I got up to go join him.

It was both a kick in the balls and not surprising in the least to see him stuffing clothes into a duffel bag and still refusing to look at me.

I cleared my throat. "Can we talk about this?"

"There's nothing to talk about." He shoved a couple pairs of jeans into the bag. Only then did he finally look at me, and it was little more than a fleeting glance through his lashes. "I'm surprised you're here."

I wanted to ask where else he thought I'd be, but I knew, and I didn't want to fight that fight. Not now. This was about us, not Jason.

Sighing, I folded my arms loosely and pressed my shoulder into the door frame. "I'm here. Apparently you don't want to be."

He laughed quietly and bitterly. "I don't want to play second fiddle to—"

"For fuck's sake," I snapped. "Just stop with that shit. You're not playing second fiddle to anyone." I tightened my arms across my chest. "If you want to call it quits after all this time, then do it, but don't try to pin this on me."

"Whatever helps you sleep at night." He yanked a couple of T-shirts out of a drawer and stuffed them into the bag. Then he zipped it so hard, I was amazed the zipper didn't snap right off, and he hauled it up onto his shoulder. As he headed for the door, I got out of the way, but I followed him up the hall.

"Are you serious?" I said to his back. "That's it? You're just—"

"Don't act like I'm wrong, Ahmed." He didn't turn around.

"You *are* wrong, damn it! Would you just fucking *talk* to me?"

He spun around so abruptly, I almost crashed into him, and he glared at me. "There's nothing to talk about. You can play stupid all you want, but you've been into him for a long, long time, and—"

"No, I haven't!" I couldn't keep the exasperation out of my voice. "And if it's been a thing for a long time, why haven't you said anything until now? You haven't said a single fucking word until you're already on your way out the door. *Why didn't you say anything?*"

He pressed his lips together and held my gaze, anger flashing in his eyes.

Then he turned and continued down the hall. "I'm done."

A dozen arguments made it to the tip of my tongue, but they didn't get any further than that. If he was this determined to leave, then…what was the point of arguing? He didn't want to be with someone he thought wanted someone else. I didn't want to be with someone who didn't want to be with me. Or who was *that* convinced I wanted to cheat on him.

So I watched in silence as he shoved his feet into his shoes and put his jacket back on. Then he pulled the bag onto his shoulder again, and…

Left.

The door slammed shut. My heart slammed into my ribs.

Numb, I sank onto the couch as the sudden silence of the apartment rang in my ears.

What the fuck just happened?

And what did it say that, just like when I'd left Mark to wait for the tow, my first impulse was to call Jason?

That was probably because I knew to my core that he'd be here in a heartbeat. No questions asked. As quickly as physics and traffic laws allowed, he'd walk through my front door, and he'd pull me into one of those hugs that made the whole world okay, and just thinking about that had my eyes stinging with tears that *didn't* have Mark's name all over them. I was hurt and angry over Mark, but this sudden longing for human contact—this sudden bone-deep need for warmth and affection—was all about Jason. I craved his hugs. His humor. The way he always knew when a joke wasn't welcome and when I desperately needed to smile.

He couldn't fix this. He couldn't take away the heartache Mark had left behind. But he could be here, and without even saying a word, he could make me believe this wouldn't last forever.

I just lost my boyfriend. I need my friend.

But he'd already been a saint this weekend, scraping Mark and me up off the side of the road when he could've just been enjoying a piece of pie at the café. He was always there with an ear and a shoulder, whether because Mark and I had been in a fight or because I was struggling after a patient received an upsetting diagnosis.

Sitting back against the couch and exhaling into the stillness of my apartment, I realized I depended on Jason too much. He deserved better than constantly dropping everything to help me.

And on top of that, I couldn't help feeling guilty for this impulse to run to the man Mark insisted was pulling me away from him. I knew on some level that Mark was just gaslighting me. That, or he was imagining things. Jason was a dear friend, but I was nothing if not a faithful boyfriend. It didn't matter how Jason felt about me. He couldn't steal me from Mark unless I wanted to be stolen, and no matter what Mark thought he was seeing, I *didn't* want to be stolen.

No, the only reason I wanted to run to Jason right now was for support. For *friendship*.

And maybe for someone to tell me it was normal to be hurt and angry over my boyfriend leaving, but also to feel this profound sense of relief.

Because…

Because I *was* relieved.

The slamming door had let me release my breath.

I suddenly felt like I was getting back my life. My freedom.

What the fuck was I supposed to make of that?

CHAPTER 5

Jason

"*M*ake sure you finish all of the antibiotics." I tapped my stylus on the tablet in my hand. "It's a ten-day supply, and it's super important you take all of them, even if you're feeling better."

Mrs. Gray nodded, wincing as she swallowed. "I know," she croaked. "I've taken them before."

"Okay." I smiled. "Dr. Bauer has already submitted the prescription to your pharmacy, so just swing by the front desk to make sure all your insurance ducks are in a row, and you're done. I hope you feel better soon."

She returned my smile with a weak but genuine one. "I will. Thanks, honey."

I left the exam room and triple-checked the iPad in case there were any loose ends. Nope, looked good, so I closed out her appointment and switched to my next one on the schedule.

"Hey, Jason?" Rachel, the office manager, leaned out of

her office. "Ahmed's not here yet. You and Kim are going to have to shoulder everything until he gets in."

My stomach flipped. "Sure, but he is coming in, right? Is he okay?"

"He's trying." She checked her phone and scowled. "Car trouble, I guess."

"No shit? Man, those two can't win for losing when it comes to cars this week."

"Oh yeah?"

I nodded as I skimmed the details of my next appointment on the iPad. "Mark hit something on the way home from that carnival the other night. Busted his axle, I think."

"Yikes." She grimaced. "That sounds expensive."

"Yep. Hopefully Ahmed's car didn't decide to outdo it."

"Let's hope. I'll keep you posted when I hear from him."

"Cool. And don't worry about the patients—Kim and I can handle it."

That got a grateful, if tired smile from Rachel. "You're the best."

I flashed her another smile, and as she returned to her office, I went looking for Kim to divvy up patients. I would absolutely never complain about filling in for a coworker (after all, they'd done the same for me millions of times, and anyway, shit happened). But the truth was, this clinic was busy as hell. When we were down a nurse, chaos could descend in short order, especially if we got an emergency walk-in or someone took more time than they'd been allotted.

That second thing happened... Well, pretty much always, since insurance companies were still deluding themselves into thinking patients only needed fifteen-minute appointment slots. Right. Because that was totally enough time for taking vitals, listening to concerns, conveying information to one of the doctors, performing examinations, answering questions, and all that other frivolous stuff we liked to do just to fleece insurance companies.

So it wasn't like we could prevent the office from running late thanks to patients going over their allotted time. We could just manage the workload as much as possible to minimize the situation while still providing the care patients needed. Shame we were limited by things like, I don't know, physics and reality.

Ah well. Such was the job.

Kim and I kept things moving, and I thought we did a pretty good job. We held down the fort, and by the time the medical assistant and office staff were peeling away for their breaks, we were only running about twenty minutes behind.

Around ten-thirty, as I was closing out a patient's appointment, Ahmed came shuffling in. I didn't even get a chance to be relieved that he was here before my heart dropped. He looked utterly wrung out. As if he hadn't slept at all since the other night, and he was more flustered and stressed than I'd seen him in ages. In this line of work, that said a lot. He was put together and could probably smile and be professional, but his beard looked scruffier than it ever did at work, his complexion had paled a shade or two, and his eyes were... Fuck. *Something* was wrong, that was for sure.

"Hey." I lowered my tablet. "Everything okay?"

He sighed and leaned against the wall. "Not really."

Alarm had the hairs on my neck standing on end. "Come on." I gently took his elbow and herded him toward his office. He did a lot of administrative work, so he had his own office rather than the communal desks the rest of us used. One of the other nurses had gotten bent out of shape over that at one point, but then she realized that Ahmed could take a ton of crap off all of our plates and get it done efficiently and accurately if he had a place to do it with no distractions. Him having his own office was the tradeoff for the sheer volume of work he did in addition to caring for patients, and we were all grateful for it.

In the office, he put his laptop case on his chair, and he started pulling things out and putting them on his desk. Without preamble, he said, "Mark and I broke up."

My knees actually wobbled. "You… Seriously?"

Ahmed didn't look at me. He tossed the painting he'd won the other night onto his closed laptop, then put the bag on the floor beside his desk. Dropping into the now-vacant chair, he sighed, sounding absolutely wrung out. "We just… I don't even know. It was like we were both wiped out after that whole debacle getting home from the carnival, and then we started fighting, and it…" He rolled his hand. "Escalated."

"Escalated?" I stared at him. "From arguing about the carnival to breaking up?"

"Kind of. I guess. I don't know." He wiped a hand over his face, skin scuffing audibly over his beard. "Just…it's over. That's all there really is to say. He's staying with his sister for the moment, and he's moving out as soon as he locks something down."

"Whoa. I'm…" It felt like a lie to say I was sorry to see Mark go. And it would be, because Ahmed deserved way better. But I *was* sorry to see Ahmed this upset, so I told him that. "Is there anything I can do?"

He shook his head. "Nah. I just have to let this part run its course." He laughed bitterly. "And then, on top of *all* of that, I blow a tire on the way to work this morning."

I whistled. "Jesus, dude. Were you able to fix it?"

"It's at the repair shop right now." He sat back and ran a hand through his thick, black hair. "And I should've been here ages ago. I should've been able to just change the damn tire, drive to the shop on the doughnut, and then Uber to work, but *nooo*"—he laughed again, rolling his eyes—"I had to wait for a fucking tow truck because the damn doughnut was flat, too."

"What?" I gaped at him. "How does that even happen?"

Ahmed threw up his hands. "Who knows? It's..." He paused. Then he shook his head. "Anyway. I'm late as fuck." He rubbed the back of his neck gingerly, as if every muscle were stiff and sore. "I'll be fine. Where are we with patients?"

I hesitated, momentarily worried he wasn't in any frame of mind to be seeing patients. But this was Ahmed. He could rally from almost anything in order to be what a patient needed, and he was the first to tap out when he thought he was too tired or otherwise not up to the job.

Still, I said, "You'll say so if you need a break, right? You're dealing with a lot."

"I know." He smiled, which somehow made him look even more exhausted. "I'll be fine. If nothing else, I can handle taking vitals and free up you and Kim to deal with the rest."

That was fair. Ahmed and I both joked that we could do vitals in our sleep.

"All right. Just say so." I took my iPad out from under my arm. "There's a patient in six who's following up two weeks post-op." I tapped the screen. "Her info is on your tablet."

He checked his tablet, then nodded sharply and flashed me another quick, tired smile. We left his office to continue with our workday.

As the afternoon wore on, I had to wonder if I was more distracted than he was. Ahmed could handle a lot of things. He kept a cool head like few others—I'd seen it myself, and I'd heard some stories from a nurse who used to work here and had done emergency department rotations with him in school. He was born for this job, and I wished I had half his ability to operate at a hundred percent when, by all rights, he should've been facedown on the floor.

But everyone had their limits. No matter how much I

couldn't stand Mark, the breakup was obviously taking its toll on Ahmed. They'd been together like five years. Splitting up meant some serious upheaval. That, on top of the cascade of car trouble, was bound to leave him threadbare.

I didn't think he was a danger to our patients. He knew when to cry *"uncle!"* and step back for patient safety.

I was just worried sick that he didn't know when to quit for his own sake.

While Ahmed went into another exam room, I pulled Kim aside. "Hey, Ahmed's here, but he's got a lot on his plate. Let's keep his patient load down as much as possible today."

She frowned. "That means loading us both up for the next several hours."

"I know." I exhaled, tired just from imagining the rest of the day. "But he pulls more than his own weight around here —the least we can do is return the favor until he's back on all eight cylinders."

Kim nodded, her gaze drifting toward Ahmed's office. Then she looked up at me and smiled. "Guess we can give the workhorse an easy day today. God knows he's earned it."

I didn't imagine anything about today would be easy for Ahmed.

But I'd take it.

"ARE YOU FUCKING *KIDDING* ME?"

Ahmed's frustration had every head turning toward his office door. The clinic was closed, so there were no patients within earshot, but there were still nurses and office staff hanging around to catch up on notes, clean equipment, and refill supplies in each exam room in between resting exhausted bodies before our evening commutes.

We all exchanged wide-eyed looks, and every gaze finally landed on me. The room was loud with an unspoken, *"Are you going to go check on him?"*

Hell yes, I was.

I got up, ignoring the ache in my back and knees from seeing patient after patient after patient today, and crossed the room to his open door. Cautiously, I poked my head into his office, where I found him staring at his laptop. "Uh, everything okay?"

Ahmed leaned back in his chair and waved a hand at the laptop. "It's completely fried."

"What?" I stepped inside so I had a better look at the screen. "Fried how?"

"It crashed on me, and now it won't boot up. Nothing happens. I did a hard restart, but then it got seriously hot. I… Ugh, I'm going to call tech support, but I doubt there's anything we can do."

Judging by the distinctly acrid smell of burnt electronics, it was probably toast. Hopefully the only thing fried was the power supply, and maybe the computer itself could be salvaged.

Ahmed sighed. "I guess I'll leave myself a note to call first thing in the morning." He reached for a pen, but he paused and picked up the painting he'd won at the carnival instead. With a tired, humorless laugh, he said, "Between the cars, the breakup, and now the laptop, I swear this stupid thing is cursed or something." Then his brow furrowed as he peered at the carousel horses, and his tone turned serious. "Shit. Maybe it really *is* cursed."

I cocked my head. All right, now I knew he was running on fumes, because Ahmed was the most skeptical, rational person on the planet. He didn't believe in luck, curses, superstition—any of it. "Cursed?" I ventured carefully.

"Makes as much sense as anything else." He stared at the

painting for a long moment before turning an unreadable look on me. "Am I going insane? Because I'm really starting to think this thing is cursed."

"I don't think you're going insane. I think your world has been yanked out from under you from like six different directions, and anyone would be looking for some way to make it all make sense."

"Maybe. I don't know." Ahmed paused for a long moment, pursing his lips as he glared at the painting. "Eh." He tossed it in the trashcan beside his desk and chuckled as he said, "Why take chances?"

I wasn't going to judge. Anything to make him feel better right now was cool with me. "I'm down with not taking chances. In fact"—I gestured at the trashcan—"We could make sure it's gone for good. Go bury it in the woods or some shit."

Ahmed laughed halfheartedly. "With the way my week is going, we'd stumble across a body, and the police would pin it on me somehow."

"I'll be your alibi!" I flashed him a toothy grin. "I'll tell them the truth—we were in the woods, burying an unlucky painting, and just happened to stumble across—"

A much more enthusiastic laugh poured out of him, and he leaned back in his desk chair. "Oh God. I can just see them taking down *that* statement." He adopted a comical scowl. "Mr. Kazimi, do you really expect us to believe you were burying a painting? And your shovel hit a bone, and now here we are?"

"But if that's what happened!" I put up my hands. "People find bodies all the time but aren't suspects."

"Yeah, but like I said, with the way my week has been going..." He trailed off. Then he made a face. "Would you think I was nuts if I said I'd feel better taking it out to the dumpster myself instead of just throwing it in here?" He leaned down, pulled out the trash bag, and started tying it closed. "Because I think I might be insane, but I really, *really* want to be as far away from this thing as I can get."

It didn't even matter what I believed about curses or anything else—I couldn't stand seeing Ahmed this worked up and stressed out.

"I say toss it," I told him. "Worst-case scenario, you'll feel kind of silly. Best-case, you'll feel better. So why not?"

He watched me uncertainly, as if he were expecting me to drop a punchline or some kind of backhanded remark.

The only comment that came to the tip of my tongue was that he'd clearly been with Mark too damn long. I was his friend. He was hanging by a thread. Why would I rip on him for doing whatever harmless thing he needed to do—no matter how irrational it was—so he could breathe easier?

"Let's go." I gestured over my shoulder. "I'll empty a couple of cans from the other desks, too, and we can get it all out of here."

That brought a smile to his face, and his shoulders visibly relaxed, as did his features. "Okay. Sounds good."

We gathered up trash bags from the front desks as well as the ones I shared with the other nurses. We could only carry so much, and of course we didn't touch the sharps or biohazards—a service would come by in the morning to collect those—but between us, we walked out with six bags. If nothing else, it would make the night cleaning crew's job easier, so I wouldn't lose any sleep over it.

At the dumpster, we tossed all the bags over except one. Ahmed paused with that last one hanging from his fist, and we both peered warily at it.

The painting was easy to see. Through the thin white plastic, the hard lines and even some of the colors showed through, and the corners strained at the bag like some alien creature trying to pierce a membrane and break free.

Damn. I wasn't creeped out by the painting per se, but right then…yeah, I kinda was.

Ahmed shuddered. "Good riddance." Then he heaved the bag over the lip of the dumpster, and it landed with a thud and some crinkling. Dusting off his hands, he chuckled. "Would setting it all on fire be overkill?"

I laughed as we headed back toward the clinic. "I mean, maybe? But it would probably also get you…well, fired. And I think you're trying to *stop* all the bad luck, right?"

"Hmm, you make a good point." He glanced over his shoulder. "Except there's also a bag of pamphlets in there from that one pharma rep who keeps trying to peddle those liver-destroying allergy meds. So it would be cleansing fire, you know?"

I threw a glance at the dumpster myself, pursing my lips, then stopped to pull open the clinic door. As he walked in ahead of me, I said, "Okay, I'm tempted. I really am. But they have those cameras outside, and last I heard, arson looks really bad on a résumé."

"Ugh. *Fine.*" Ahmed sighed theatrically as we headed up the hallway to our clinic door. "Gotta get five-star patient reviews. Gotta be nice to the drug reps." He gestured behind us. "Can't set a fire in the dumpster in the parking lot. I swear, this job gets harder and harder every year."

I just chuckled, relieved that he was snarking and being ridiculous again. He was probably still losing his mind over his breakup, his car, and now his work laptop being fried, but he was closer to himself than he'd been before we'd made the trash run. I'd take it.

At our clinic's door, though, he paused and turned to me, renewed fatigue radiating off him. "Thank you. For humoring me."

"Don't worry about it." I gently reeled him into a hug, and as he leaned into me and sighed, I added, "With as much as you've got going on, I'll support whatever you need to feel better."

"Thanks." He returned my embrace. After a moment, he stepped back and absently ran a hand through his hair, oblivious to what that did to my body temperature. "They say bad shit comes in threes. Let's hope I've hit the trifecta with Mark, the cars, and the laptop. Because I don't know how much more I can take."

"Let's hope. But you've got support. Don't ever forget that."

A soft smile broke through the exhaustion. "You're the best."

Then he turned to head into the clinic, and I stole a second to stare at his back and wish I could do so, so much more for him. Right then, I'd have gladly set that dumpster's contents on fire, damage to my career be damned, just to take some weight off Ahmed's tired shoulders.

You deserve nothing but happiness, I wanted to tell him. *I hope that's exactly what you find after all this bullshit.*

Then I followed him into the clinic to see if we could salvage his laptop.

CHAPTER 6

Ahmed

*T*he night we all went to the carnival, I'd basically fallen in love with that weird prize from the button game. It was so different and seriously cool right up until I'd decided it was cursed.

And admittedly, I was sad that I didn't have it anymore. Especially since I felt stupid for convincing myself it was cursed in the first place. Curses didn't exist. Objects didn't bring bad energy or bad luck or whatever. They were just inanimate objects. I'd overreacted because I'd been a mess over all the bullshit suddenly happening in my life. I'd abandoned rationality, and now I was never going to see that little painting again. Plus the river of bullshit hadn't exactly ceased to flow after I'd tossed the prize in the trash.

So, I can't lie: three days, some more car trouble, a few hours on the phone trying to get some fraudulent charges removed from my credit card, and a fritzed-out washing machine later...I felt really stupid. *And* I missed that painting.

But holy shit, that did *not* mean I was happy to see it again.

For long seconds, I stared at it, trying to make sense of how the ever-loving fuck it had ended up on my kitchen counter.

I was just here. Literally five minutes ago, I'd been in here, cleaning out my lunch bag and dishes. My lunch bag had been sitting in that exact spot. Then I'd hung it on its hook, grabbed my keys, and gone downstairs to check my mail, since my hands had been full when I'd come in from the car.

Now I was back in my kitchen, the mail still in my hand, and there it was—that strange painting of the carousel horse, complete with the stains where the "potion" had desaturated the colors.

"What the fuck..." I breathed into the silence of my kitchen.

A prank. It had to be. Mark still had a key, since he was still moving out. But I knew for a fact he was at work right now—he'd called to bitch at me about something as I was pulling into the parking lot, and I knew the background noise of his job like I knew my own. Plus he had no idea I'd thrown the painting away, never mind that I'd thrown it into the dumpster at work.

A few of our friends had keys for various reasons, including Jason and Lucas. Maybe they'd fished it out of the trash at work, held on to it, and then snuck in here and planted it on my counter to freak me out?

Except...no. Jason had seemed a little creeped out by the painting, too, and while he and Lucas both liked to joke around, it would be wildly out of character for either of them to commit hard enough to a prank that they'd go dumpster diving. Least of all in a dumpster used by a medical facility, since you didn't work in a place like that without developing some healthy paranoia about improperly discarded sharps and biohazards.

And there was still the part where there had been nothing on that counter when I'd gone downstairs. Nothing. Because my lunch bag had been there, and then I'd moved it, and I distinctly remembered wiping some crumbs off the completely empty counter before I'd gone down to check the mail.

So unless someone was in my apartment...

The hair on my neck stood up. All logistics about retrieving the painting aside, now I was really paranoid, and I quickly swept every room and hidden corner of my apartment like a cop during a raid.

Okay, maybe not like a cop. More like the freaked-out character in a horror movie who's hyperventilating and peeking around corners, sure there's an axe murderer at every turn.

Spoiler: there was no axe murderer in my apartment.

There was no one in my apartment except for me.

I returned to the kitchen and leaned against the counter opposite where the painting sat. For a long time, I stared at it as I tried to make sense of how exactly it had gotten here. After all, there had to be a rational explanation that didn't involve curses, ghosts, or...like...space aliens or something.

Maybe I wasn't remembering something correctly. I'd taken multiple bags of trash out that day. Was it possible I'd forgotten to make sure the painting was actually in one of them?

No, because I distinctly remembered its corners trying to poke through the bag and one of the carousel horses eyeing me creepily through the thin white plastic.

Damn. I really should've set that stupid dumpster on fire. Yeah, I probably would've lost my job and gone to jail or something, but given how things had been going this week, that was probably going to find a way to happen anyway.

I glared at the painting. I didn't have to set a dumpster on fire, but I could burn *that* thing to ash.

Yes. That was what I'd do. Kill it with fire. Then I'd be absolutely sure it was fucking *gone*. And I'd video it burning, too. I was taking *no* chances this time.

Filled with determination and maybe still just a bit creeped out, I gathered everything I needed—the painting, some junk mail I hadn't gotten around to tossing, my phone, and my keys. Then I headed for the parking lot.

I swung into a convenience store along the way and picked up the remaining essentials. Lighter fluid. A pack of three lighters in case one didn't work. Some newspapers because I wasn't fucking around. Two gallons of water because I didn't want to start a wildfire.

Then I drove out to a park where the clinic had its annual Fourth of July barbecue. At one end was an area where people could park RVs, camp, and hold cookouts, and I even stopped to buy a permit because…taking no chances.

At my designated spot, I got to work. I made a thick nest of newspaper in the firepit and doused it with lighter fluid. At its center, I tucked the painting, gave it a generous coat of lighter fluid, and added some more newspaper around its edges.

I had to laugh when I stepped back to inspect my handiwork. It looked like it was a few candles and a pentagram shy of a ritual sacrifice. Fine. I didn't care what it looked like now as long as there was nothing left but ash when I was done.

I opened one of the water jugs and saturated the ground around the firepit. The other I kept nearby just in case the fire decided to get cute.

With my phone propped up and filming, I rolled a piece of newspaper until it resembled a ten-inch blunt covered in ads for overpriced furniture. Then I flicked the lighter at its end. The edges of the paper curled away from the flame, but soon it was ablaze. I blew on it gently to encourage the fire, and once it was burning, I touched it to the nest in the firepit.

Just like I'd hoped, it all went up quickly and dramatically. In the time it took me to grab my phone and bring it in closer, the fire had consumed most of the paper and started aggressively dancing over the painting. For a few panicked seconds, I was afraid the painting might survive. That it had been coated in some kind of fire retardant—or hell, a hex, because I wasn't discounting anything—and would just lie there and laugh at me while the newspaper turned to ash.

But then the fire started digging in, making the edges glow and darken as it melted the paint and blurred the image.

I swore the spots that had been desaturated by the potion burned blue instead of orange. Weird, but whatever—it was burning, and the flames quickly chewed through the paint and ate away at the edges of the thin board.

The heat was intense, making my face feel sunburned, but I didn't step away. I didn't care if I was sweaty or if I was seeing afterimages once the fire died down—I wanted to watch and film until that damn thing was gone for good.

By the time the flames ran out of fuel and began to die down, the evening had started to dim as well. Or it might've just seemed that way since I'd been staring into the fire for however long. Fine. The end result was a pile of ash in the firepit.

Juuust to be on the safe side, I waited until the fire had died away, and then I put down paper and lighter fluid and lit another one. When this fire had finally died, the night was dark, and an inspection with my phone's flashlight revealed nothing but black-and-white ash. No fragments of newspaper. No scraps of the painting. Nothing at all except the barely there remnants of some logs someone else had put down here for a campfire or a barbecue.

That was when it dawned on me that whoever came here next might cook food on this firepit. I had no way of knowing what was in the paint or the board of the painting, but I was pretty sure some paints contained things like cobalt, lead, and cadmium. Probably not something I should've been breathing in, and not something I should leave for the next campers.

I probably looked like an absolute lunatic, scooping ashes into plastic shopping bags. At this point, I didn't really care what I looked like or how far out of my mind I'd gone. This painting—this stupid carnival prize—needed to die in a fire, and I needed to make sure the ashes were destroyed and discarded too.

Rational? Doubt it.

But I'd thrown the damn thing out, and it had materialized on my kitchen counter, so rational could go straight to hell.

Once I'd cleaned up that firepit until there was nothing left but dirt and ashes that were probably older than I was, I gathered up the bags and took them to the park's trash bins. As luck would have it, the truck was going around to empty them, and I waited to make sure everything wound up in its bed. The guys shot me puzzled expressions, but I didn't care what they thought of me.

I just cared that that stupid painting was burned, burned *again*, bagged, and fucking *gone*.

Dusting off my hands, I headed back to my car. In the driver seat, I watched the video. Over and over, I watched the painting dissolve into nothing. I sent it to Jason, too, and he replied with, *How the fuck did you find that thing again?*

Fair question. I didn't explain that it had found me, and I just said, *No idea, but it's gone for good this time.*

Then I watched the video one more time for good measure.

It's gone, Ahmed, I told myself. *Go home.*

Breathing a sigh of relief, I put my phone on the passenger seat.

And I drove home, leaving the remains of the painting far, far behind.

Some of your stuff got mixed up with mine. I can bring it by tonight.

I sighed as I read Mark's text. It wasn't surprising—neither of us had wanted to let the grass grow on him moving out, so things were bound to wind up in the wrong places. As it was, I had a couple of boxes of odds and ends he'd left behind. The sooner we exchanged the remaining pieces of our former life, the sooner we could move on.

I just didn't relish seeing him again. This had already been the week from hell. Having Mark in the apartment again wasn't going to make that any better.

What if he picks a fight?

Or what if...

Ugh, if he wants sex, I will legit throw up on him.

It wasn't even surreal to feel that way about him. It was like I'd always been disgusted by him and wanted to get away from him, even though I could clearly remember periods of being ridiculously in love with him. I could remember pretty good sex with the man whose touch would make me dry heave now.

Breakups were fucking weird. Though this one had fallen

out of the clear blue sky and caught me completely off-guard, there was nothing I could do to change Mark's mind. I really didn't want to anymore, honestly. So now that there was no stopping it, I'd decided that the sooner it was over, the better.

I was nervous answering the door when he arrived. Facing each other as fresh exes could be a minefield after the most amicable of breakups, so there was no telling how this would go.

To my surprise—and relief—he acknowledged me with a nod and a "Hey" before he handed me a couple of boxes. Then he came in and took off his shoes while I put the boxes down in the living room. Apparently we'd already passed the angry sniping stage and had moved on to being frostily polite. Civil, but not exactly friendly. I'd take it.

I looked through one of the boxes, double-checking that everything was mine, and also on that off chance something jogged my memory about something else that might've been lost in the shuffle. Mark did the same with the boxes I'd brought out for him, pawing through the contents with a scowl on his face.

There was nothing amiss in my boxes. Some clothes. A pair of sneakers. Some of my nursing school textbooks, which I remembered now had been on the same shelf as his engineering books. There was also a bottle of cologne that had probably ended up on his side of the bathroom counter. He'd thoughtfully put it in a Ziploc bag, too; thank God for that, since I didn't need everything I owned smelling like Hugo Boss.

I stacked the boxes in the hallway so I could empty them later, then went back to the living room to ask if Mark needed a hand hauling everything down to his car.

As I stepped into the room, Mark was leaning down, reaching deep into a box. "This," he said, "is definitely not mine." He fished something out and tossed it on the coffee table.

And my feet and heart both stopped as the item landed beside the TV remote in a puff of black dust.

Beneath smears of soot, the carousel horse's eye peered back at me.

"Oh, goddammit." Mark huffed with annoyance as he tried to dust off his hands, succeeding only in getting soot all over everything. "What the fuck is—oh, shit. It's on everything!"

My stomach lurched up into my throat. "I'm… Sorry. I have no idea how that got in there."

"Yeah, but what the fuck is *on* it?" He angrily showed his hands, and they were almost as black as mine had been after I'd scooped all the ash out of the firepit last night. "What *is* this shit?"

"I…" I shook my head. "I don't know. If you want to change into something, I can wash your—oh, fuck. I'm still waiting for a new washing machine."

"A new washing machine?" He cocked his head. "What happened to the old one?"

I made an irritated noise and gestured toward the back room where the washer and dryer lived. "Crapped out. New one's coming next week."

Mark blinked, startled enough that he seemed to have forgotten about the soot all over his hands and clothes. "Oh. Damn. Do you, uh…" He turned a sheepish look on me. "It was mine, too. Do you need help with it?"

Truthfully? Yeah, I could've used some help with buying a new damn washer on top of fixing my car. But that would just mean more interactions with Mark, and I'd rather eat ramen for a few months. Plus I doubted he had the extra money while he was working on getting a new place and he'd had to cough up money for his own car. It would be less headache to handle it myself.

"I've got it," I croaked. "Don't worry about it."

He studied me skeptically, then shrugged. When he glanced down, his irritation returned. "For fuck's sake. Can I at least…" He motioned toward the bathroom.

I nodded mutely, and he brushed past me. I didn't even care that he'd probably leave the sink covered in soot, and he'd probably get it on the towels, too. We'd argued about stuff like that forever, mostly him bitching at me for daring to leave a single beard trimming or two in the sink. If he left a mess in there… Whatever. I didn't have the energy to care about it tonight.

Especially not when I was suddenly laser-focused on…*that.*

Warily, I crept toward the coffee table. This was straight up impossible. The only explanation was that Mark must've gone back to the carnival, played the game again, and won another one.

Which totally explained the desaturated spots on this one, right? The splatter marks in the exact same places that had glowed blue last night? When I'd *burned the fucking thing to ash?*

I hadn't imagined that, had I? Had I dreamed about it?

No, in fact I'd *videoed* it.

I yanked my phone out of my back pocket and shakily thumbed to my photo and video library.

There was no video.

I mean, there was. The file was still there. When I hit Play, the timer ran as if a video were playing. There was just no picture. No sound. The screen was black. There wasn't even any static or anything like that. Literally nothing.

"What the hell?" I murmured.

"Huh?" Mark's voice turned me around, and our eyes

locked as he came into the living room, wiping his hands on his jeans. "You say something?"

"I, uh…" I glanced at my screen. He wouldn't believe me if I told him—I didn't even believe it, and I doubted any rational person would. So I just shook my head and pocketed my phone. "Text from work. They need to me to come in early this week." A believable lie, considering how often the clinic did ask me to come in early or stay late.

Mark grunted. "You'd think they'd just hire someone if they don't have enough nurses to cover everything."

I laughed halfheartedly, my skin still crawling from the reappearing painting and the vanishing video. "Yeah, but why do that when they can just get me to pick up the slack?"

I regretted it as soon as I said it; Mark had ranted many, many times about the clinic taking advantage of me, squeezing extra hours out of me without paying me more, and me being a pushover.

But he just shrugged and picked up one of the boxes. "I'm going to run this down to the car. Back in a minute for the rest."

"Sure. Do you need me to…?" I gestured at the remaining two.

"Nah. I've got it." He put the box down by the door, slipped his shoes back on, and headed out to the parking lot.

Alone in the apartment, I stared at the soot-smeared painting.

I'd thrown it in the dumpster at work.

It reappeared.

I'd burned it. I'd *filmed* it burning.

It was back again.

What in the ever-loving fuck was happening?

CHAPTER 7

Jason

"If she seems really uncomfortable," I told the young mother, "Tylenol should help." I handed her a small card. "This has recommended dosages and any symptoms you want to watch out for."

She took the card in her free hand—her eighteen-month-old was curled against her other shoulder, still crying softly after her vaccination. The mother gave the card a glance, then tucked it in her purse and patted her baby's back. "She's usually fussy for a little while after, but she's never had any reactions before. Knock on wood."

I smiled. "Well, just keep an eye on her, and give us a call if you have any questions or concerns."

"I will. Thank you." She headed up front to settle up her copay, and I went to my desk to close out her visit.

Leaning against one of the other desks, Lucas was staring at his cell phone, his features taut with worry and fatigue.

I inclined my head. "Hey. Everything okay?"

Lucas sighed and sat back, putting his phone facedown on the desk. "It's Tina."

"Oh yeah? What's up?"

He rubbed the bridge of his nose, then made a tired, frustrated gesture. "She keeps waking up with these awful headaches. She called in sick to work again today, but she won't let me even try to figure out what's wrong."

I pursed my lips. "Wants you to be the fiancé, not the doctor?"

"Pretty much." He shook his head and sighed again. "She's convinced I'm hearing hoofbeats and thinking zebras, but she won't even give me a chance to see if it's horses, you know?"

I nodded slowly. "Has she talked to her actual doctor?"

"She doesn't think she needs to. Says it's her sinuses, or…" His shoulders sagged, worry coming off him in waves. "I just wish she'd let *someone* check her, you know?"

"Yeah, I bet. Well, good luck. Hopefully it's just the weather or something. My allergies have been a nightmare all summer, so…"

He nodded. "Yeah. Mine, too. But this doesn't seem…" He trailed off, eyes unfocused. Then he shook himself, picked up his phone, and slid it into the pocket of his lab coat. "I should get to work. I've got patients waiting."

"Okay. Just say so if you need me to pick up anything." There wasn't a ton I could do that I didn't already, since I wasn't an M.D., but sometimes if he fell behind, I'd close out his charts or enter some of his notes, prescriptions, or referral requests for him.

"Thanks." He picked up his iPad and furrowed his brow.

"Your nine o'clock is in five," I told him. "I already saw him, so everything should be in his chart for you."

Lucas swiped something, then nodded sharply and flashed me a tired smile. "It's all right here. Thanks, Jason!"

"Don't mention it."

He headed down the hall to see his patient. I watched him go, worry coiling in the pit of my stomach. It sucked sometimes, being frustratingly and perpetually single, but there were times when I didn't envy my partnered friends and colleagues. On the other hand, I wished I had someone I cared about enough to worry over like Lucas worried over Tina.

Well. I could fire up the old dating profile this evening. For now, I had patients waiting, and—

"Hey, Jason?" Ahmed's voice always stopped me in my tracks, but the undercurrent of panic had my heart in my throat. When I turned around, he had an expression I'd never seen before. Was that what people meant when they said someone looked like they'd seen a ghost? Because I was pretty sure Ahmed had lost a couple of shades of color, and his eyes were huge.

Alarm surged through me. "What's up?"

He gestured into his office. Puzzled and definitely worried, I followed him.

"Close the door," he said over his shoulder as he put his laptop case on his chair.

Weird, but all right. I glanced at the time—I could spare maybe ten minutes before the schedule started getting backlogged—and then nudged the door shut behind me.

"Okay." He locked eyes with me as he swallowed hard. "I need you to tell me if I'm crazy."

I blinked. "Uh. What?"

He took a deep breath. "The other day. I sent you that video, right?"

"The video?" But then it clicked. "Oh, the one of you burning the painting? Yeah, why?"

Ahmed exhaled and sagged back against his desk. "So you saw it. You remember it. Right?"

85

I cocked my head. "Yes? Why?"

He opened his bag, reached inside, and then withdrew…

The painting.

The same one he'd filmed himself burning. I wanted to ask if he'd gone back to the carnival and won another one or something, but the soot all over it…and on his hands…

My lips parted. "The fuck?"

"I know, right?" Ahmed chafed his arms, leaving a smudge of soot on the sleeve of his scrubs. "And the fucked-up thing? Mark found it. In the boxes of stuff he was moving out of my place. Boxes *I* packed. *Before* I burned that thing."

"He—*how?*"

"I don't know. I don't… It's…" Ahmed blew out a breath. "Do you still have the video?"

"I should." I fumbled with my phone and opened our chat. I scrolled back to where he'd sent me the file. "Yeah, it's right here." I tapped it, and—

Error. File not Found.

"What the hell?"

Ahmed straightened. "What?"

I showed him the error message. Then I went into my saved photos and videos. I found the file, but it wouldn't open at all. "What the…"

"It's gone from my mine, too," he breathed. "I mean, it's there, but it's just… there's nothing. It's like a blank screen with no sound."

"Fucking hell," I whispered.

"Right? And like… God, I've had the weirdest and worst luck ever since I got that thing, and now I can't fucking get rid of it. I…" He threw up his hands. "What the hell do I do?"

I stared at the painting like it might come to life and attack one of us. My skin crawled and my stomach roiled; I'd kind of jokingly agreed it might be cursed, but now that it had rematerialized twice—once after we'd both seen it burned to ash—I was creeped the fuck out. "I have no idea what to do with it."

He leaned against the wall and laughed, sounding more exhausted and resigned than anything. "Maybe this is like a *Lord of the Rings* thing where I need to go drop it in a volcano or some shit."

"It's... Maybe?"

Ahmed eyed me. "Huh?"

"I mean, not a volcano," I clarified. "But maybe the only way to get rid of it is to take it back where it came from."

He studied me as if he couldn't decide if I were making a serious suggestion or yanking his chain. Slowly, his gaze slid toward the painting. "So...like, back to the carnival?"

"Worth a try." I paused. "Assuming it's even still here. I have no idea how long it runs."

Renewed panic rose in Ahmed's expression. "Oh, shit. What if it's gone? What if I can't get rid of—"

"Ahmed. Ahmed." I stepped closer and put my hands on his shoulders. "Breathe."

He did, inhaling slowly through his nose.

"Don't get yourself spun up about hypotheticals," I said gently. "Go out to the carnival, see if it's still there, and if it is, give it back to the guy."

He swallowed like it took some serious effort, and his voice was small and uneasy as he whispered, "But what if it's gone?"

I squeezed his shoulders before letting them go. "Then we'll figure something out."

"We?"

"Well, yeah." I shrugged. "If it really is stressing you out this much, and it's causing this much chaos in your life, I'm happy to help you unload it."

Ahmed's worried expression shifted to a tired smile. "Thanks." He checked the time on his phone. "Shit. I need to get to work. But I'm going to be a mess all day until I can get out there and—"

"If you need to go, then go." I gestured over my shoulder. "Schedule's pretty light today except for some well-baby visits and sports physicals. Kim and I can hold down the fort."

His eyes widened. "You…you think I should just go? Like now?"

"Are you going to be able to function for the next several hours until you do?"

He grimaced.

"That's what I thought." I reached for the door handle. "I'll let Kim and Rachel know. Get out of here."

He blinked, but then he snatched up the painting and shoved it back into his bag. "Thank you."

"Don't mention it."

And as he headed out of the clinic like it was on fire, I hoped like hell the carnival was still there.

CHAPTER 8

Ahmed

I felt guilty, bailing on work, especially so soon after I'd come in ridiculously late thanks to my car shitting the bed. I hated leaving my coworkers high and dry at the last minute.

Patients and colleagues alike were in good hands, though. I owed Jason big time, because he absolutely would hold down the fort. Even if Kim had been out today—hell, if Rachel had been out and Jason had needed to take over the office, too—he'd have had everything running smoothly. A little behind, sure—that was inevitable when we were down a nurse—but as smoothly as any medical clinic ever could run.

Yeah, I owed him.

And I hoped this wasn't for nothing. Not just because I'd be wasting a personal day, but because if the carnival was gone and I couldn't return the painting to its Mordor, then…

Then I didn't know what I would do.

I tapped my thumbs on the wheel as I drove too fast down the highway through farm and forest country. Every time I hit a red light or I had to slow down to let someone in front of me take a turn, I was even more sure that I wasn't going to get there in time. Something in my brain had decided that the carnival was tearing down at this very moment. Pulling down rides and booths and lights. Putting it all in crates and on trailers. Heading out of that gravel road, one rumbling diesel semi-truck at a time, toward wherever they planned to set up next.

And if it was already gone, I'd never be able to find it again. There was no website. No name. Nothing. What the fuck was I supposed to do? Hire a bloodhound that could track the scent of popcorn to whichever field they set up in next?

"Don't get yourself spun up about hypotheticals," Jason's voice echoed in my mind. *"Go out to the carnival, see if it's still there, and if it is, give it back to the guy."*

Exhaling slowly, I adjusted my grip on the wheel so my hands would stop aching. He was right. There was no point in getting myself worked up over worst-case scenarios. Didn't I tell patients that all the time? It was futile, because God knew everyone's mind went straight to disaster when things like biopsies entered the equation, but thinking positively at least made it a bit less stressful to wait for those results.

I wasn't exactly waiting for biopsy results. I was on my way to a damn carnival. But Jesus Christ, I couldn't begin to imagine what I would do if those tents and lights were gone. Even now, with miles still to go, I could feel that preemptive ball of lead forming in my stomach, ready to drop the second I made the last turn and found nothing but a muddy field.

I adjusted my grip on the wheel again, sweaty palms sliding on the smooth leather.

"Breathe," Jason had said, and I concentrated on doing exactly that. Wouldn't do any good to work myself into a

panic attack, or start hyperventilating and pass out at the wheel. Especially with the way my life was going lately, and now that I knew how painfully long it could take for a damn tow truck to get out here. I didn't feel like testing how long an ambulance would take.

The highway curved, and up ahead, there was a guardrail snaking alongside the road to keep errant vehicles from veering into a swamp. A flash of déjà vu had the hair on my neck standing on end, though I couldn't figure out why.

After a second, the wires connected.

There was a section of dried mud with some rain-worn tire tracks in it, and in my mind's eye, I saw Mark's car still sitting there. The other tracks were probably from the tow truck. I could imagine Mark and the operator standing out there, soaked to the skin, the whining motor of the winch barely audible over the hammering rain as the car slowly rolled onto the flatbed. I could see me leaning against the guardrail in the dark, watching the deserted highway and hoping someone would pass by and maybe stop to help. I could still feel the jump in my pulse when a pickup truck had broken away from the passing traffic to join us.

Jason, I distinctly remembered thinking with a rush of relief. *Oh, thank God. We can finally go home.*

All of that seemed like a lifetime ago. Probably since so much had happened since then.

I glanced at the bag on the passenger seat. The painting was tucked inside, but my skin crawled as if I'd just looked right at the creepy picture.

I needed that thing gone before even more shitty things happened in my world. I didn't want to imagine what was next, but I'd never been good at *not* doing that. Every sound in my apartment was burglars or an electrical fire. Every rattle in the car was a disintegrating crankshaft or a bone-dry oil pan. Every twinge was an undiagnosed stress fracture, an aneurysm waiting to blow, or a kidney stone biding its time for the perfect moment to wreak havoc. Hell, I didn't even need anything else to actually happen—the constant waiting-for-the-next-jump-scare-paranoia was going to drive me insane on its own.

I rolled my shoulders and shifted in the driver seat as I left that guardrail in the rearview. There probably wasn't even a curse. In retrospect, my relationship had already been on rocky ground, and a few straws in a short period of time had broken the camel's back. The fact that the painting had coming into my world at the same time was pure coincidence. The common denominator was the carnival—I'd gotten the painting there, but my boyfriend had also gotten irritated, and the drive home had landed his car in the repair shop, and that had all been too much for the thin ice I hadn't realized we were standing on. It was that simple.

Which totally explains why my *car broke down.*

And why the painting reappeared.

Twice.

I shuddered.

And I may have given the car a little bit more gas, because oh my God, I needed to get to that damn carnival, *stat*.

I was so lucky to have Jason right now. I mean, I was lucky to have him anyway. He was a great friend and colleague. He was an amazing person, and I absolutely adored him. But with the avalanche of bad luck that had come tumbling down on me lately? With my breakup? With how far out of my mind I was over this stupid painting and the possibility that curses actually existed? I didn't want to imagine how much worse all this would be without Jason's gentle reassurance.

It would've been asking way, *way* too much for a million different reasons, but I couldn't lie—I wished Jason was with me now. He'd have me laughing about something ridiculous. And if he couldn't get me to laugh, he'd be outlining exactly what we were going to do to fix this situation, and he'd be calming me down, and *then* he'd be making me laugh.

Maybe I should've held out until the end of the day at work. A bigger risk of the carnival being closed, sure, but then maybe Jason would've come along. Of course he might've said no, but he also might've said yes, and I wouldn't be doing this alone.

An unexpected lump rose in my throat, and I couldn't quite push it back.

What does it mean that I want you here so bad?

I HADN'T DRIVEN the night we'd all gone to the carnival, so I hadn't paid much attention to the landmarks, but I knew the turn into the field was just after a narrow bridge and a weekend farmer's market. When I crossed the bridge and saw the farmer's market—currently deserted except for empty booths and bare tables—my heart went into overdrive.

This was it.

One more turn, and then I'd know if I even had a shot at getting rid of this stupid painting today.

I wasn't optimistic—I'd barely seen any cars on the highway, and definitely not as much traffic as I'd expect for a carnival. I reminded myself it was a weekday, so even with the kids out of school, there wouldn't be as big of a crowd as in the evenings and on weekends. But still, there would be some increase in traffic, right?

I held my breath as I put on my signal and turned down that gravel road. There were some rolling hills here that kept the carnival from being seen from the road in the daylight, though the intense glow would definitely be visible at night.

Heart pounding, I followed the winding gravel road, and when it crested a small hill...

"Oh, thank God." The words burst out of me, and my head spun.

There it was.

A few grassy fields had been converted into dirt parking lots, with hundreds of cars lined up in rows that shot out like spokes with the carnival itself as the hub. Nestled in the center, ringed by ticket booths and people standing in lines, was the cluster of colorful peaked tents. Rides were swinging and spinning. Lights were blinking and flickering. People were moving from their cars toward the lines.

If the carnival was leaving town, they sure weren't packing it up right now.

It was here. I had time. All I had to do now was park, go in, and find that damn button game.

As soon as I got to the ticket booth, though, my heart dropped again.

Cash Only.

Shit, I'd completely forgotten. And I almost never carried cash these days.

I sheepishly met the cashier's eyes. "I don't suppose there's an ATM out here?"

She pointed to her left. "Right over there."

I followed her direction, and sure enough, tucked in between her booth and the next one, was an ATM. I thanked her and went to the machine to get cash. When I turned back, I fully expected to have to walk all the way back to the end of the line, but...

No line.

Some of the other booths had people waiting, patiently

following each other through flag-lined corrals, but for whatever reason, no one had lined up here.

Well, okay then. I stepped up to the booth again, bought a ticket, and headed inside. As I did, I glanced over my shoulder.

There were easily twenty people in line behind me.

Huh. Weird. But I wasn't interested in figuring out the psychology of why people did or didn't stand in certain lines, because I had a cursed carnival prize in my bag to return. Ideally before my life started resembling a bad *Final Destination* movie.

The other night, we'd walked around the carnival so much, including retracing our steps numerous times while we visited and revisited favorites games and booths, that the layout was more or less familiar. I knew which way to go to find the rides, the vendors, and—most importantly—the games. From there, I'd just have to look around a bit until I saw that familiar *Buttons of Mystery* banner.

But after walking in circles for a solid hour, I was more confused than I'd been throughout my pharmacology class in nursing school. Which is to say: fucking baffled beyond words.

Standing there in the flow of fairway traffic, I let my gaze drift from one game booth to another. I'd made at least a dozen circles around this part of the carnival. No sign of the button game.

It was in this area. It had to be. Had they rearranged the whole place? Maybe stuck it over by the rides or vendors just to mix things up?

I went looking in those areas, too. Then did another lap through the games.

Still nothing.

Crap. Maybe it wasn't making money? Or maybe it had

been shut down because someone had found something unhygienic in among the buttons?

I found a dart-throwing game without a line, and I walked up to the girl running it.

"Step right up!" she chirped, thrusting some darts toward me. "Pop three balloons and win a prize!"

The thought of taking another prize home from this place almost made me gag. "Uh. No. No, that's okay. I just have a question."

She lowered the darts. "Sure."

"I was here the other night, and there was a game where you, like, dig around in barrels of buttons." I pantomimed the game. "Do you—"

"Oh, Buttons of Mystery!" She smiled brightly. "That's a wonderful game!"

"It is, yeah." I pasted on a smile. "I kind of wanted to give it another try, but I can't find it. Do you know…?" I gestured around.

"Mmhmm, he's at the end of this aisle." She pointed down the aisle of game booths. "He's by the high striker and the flukey ball, around the corner on your left. If you get to the milk cans, you've gone too far."

I exhaled with more relief than someone should've had over the location of a carnival game, but I didn't apologize for it. "Thank you so much."

"Don't mention it." She glanced at some kids who were descending on her booth, holding out wads of tickets. I got out of their way, and as she started getting them set up with darts, she called out to me, "Good luck!"

Oh, I needed it. I'd had enough of the other kind of luck recently to last me a while.

I followed her directions, and in no time, I found the landmarks. The high striker, where some frat boys were trying to outscore each other with the sledgehammer. The flukey ball, which had some teenagers bitching loudly about it being rigged while a woman showed her middle-school-aged kids how to effortlessly win. The milk cans, where a group of kids was trying like hell to suss out the secret to winning.

What I didn't see was the button game.

I went around the corner. I went around the other corner. I backtracked. Again. Still nothing. What the hell?

Okay, clearly I'd missed something in her directions. Fine. I'd go back and ask her to clarify.

Feeling like an idiot—and a somewhat creeped-out idiot for reasons I couldn't quite name—I returned to her booth.

But…

She wasn't there.

A hand-painted sign announced, *Back in 10!*

The kids who'd been playing? Gone. The girl operating the game? Gone.

Fucking perfect. Now what was I supposed to do?

I asked two more game operators where to find the button game. One sent me in the same direction as the first. The other said he'd walk me there himself, thank God.

"I feel like an idiot," I said. "It shouldn't be this hard to find, should it?"

The bald, bearded guy chuckled. "You'd be surprised. Anyway, the button game is right over here." He pointed in the direction he was turning, which meant crossing a thick crowd of people passing by. I followed him, trying to keep up and keep an eye on him as I shouldered and apologized my way through the dense crowd of carnival goers.

I came out the other side, relieved to reclaim my personal space, and I hurried to catch up with my guide.

Except when I was maybe two steps away, I realized it wasn't him. Just another bald dude with a beard and overalls.

His face was all wrong, though. And the guy I'd been following had tattoos.

Okay, so I lost sight of him. Fine. He couldn't have gone far.

So I halted and scanned all the faces around me.

No bald, bearded guy. No button game.

"Are you shitting me?" I asked into the popcorn-scented air.

This was getting ridiculous. With no idea what other solution to try, I took out my phone and texted Jason: *Hey, do you remember where that game was? I swear I can't find it anywhere.*

He didn't respond right away, which didn't surprise me. It was probably on silent while he was seeing patients.

There was a ton of noise around me, so I kept my phone in my hand as I continued walking. That way I'd feel the vibration when he pinged me back, and I wouldn't miss his message.

While I waited, I made another lap around the whole damn carnival. I asked another employee to help me, and promptly lost them in the crowd just like the bearded guy.

And half an hour later, I *still* couldn't find that goddamned game.

CHAPTER 9

Jason

*W*ith Ahmed out today, we were all busy as hell. I'd jinxed us, too, when I'd told him we mostly had well-baby visits and sports physicals. Suddenly there were urgent walk-ins, and three different routine visits turned into more protracted pursuits of tests, referrals, and treatment options. Hannah, one of the three doctors, had to take off because one of her kids was heading from daycare to the emergency department with a suspected fracture to her arm.

Then we were down to one doctor for a couple of hours because Lucas had gone home to check on Tina. She'd woken up feeling awful again, and he'd been worried when she didn't answer his call. Fortunately, she was more or less all right. She'd insisted it was just her sinuses giving her a wicked headache, and she didn't need to be checked out by her fiancé or any other doctor. He'd come back to work after that, but he'd had a hell of a time concentrating. Couldn't blame him.

So the day was chaotic, and by the time I had five minutes to sit down and catch my breath, it was almost four. I sat back in my chair, giving my aching feet a break, and checked my phone.

The message from Ahmed had me sitting up straight again:

Hey, do you remember where that game was? I swear I can't find it anywhere.

I looked at the time he'd sent it compared to the time on the clock. Crap, it had been a good hour and a half. He'd probably found it by now. Hell, he was probably on his way home already, having gleefully unloaded that damned painting.

But I responded anyway: *Hey, sorry. Just now got this. It was down by that hammer game and the one where you toss the wiffle balls into baskets, wasn't it?*

He started typing almost immediately. *That's what I thought. I swear I can't find it anywhere.*

I chewed my lip. *Is it gone?*

No, that's the weird thing. I've asked people. Even had people offer to show me where it is. But it's never where they say it is. And the people with me... I can't explain it. I keep losing them in crowds and whatever. There was a pause, then, *Am I this stupid? Or am I insane?*

I winced. He was neither, but I didn't blame him for questioning anything right now. In his shoes, I'd have been doing the same.

Do you want me to come up there? I asked without really thinking. *I'm stuck here until at least 6, but if you're willing to wait for me, we can grab dinner or something and then look for the place?*

You don't have to come all the way out here.

But do you want me to?

He started typing. Stopped. Started again. I glanced at the

time. Still a couple of minutes, but I'd need to get back to work soon.

Finally, he said, *Yes?*

I sighed. That was such an Ahmed answer. He wasn't someone who liked asking people to go out of their way for him. I wondered how much of that was just who he was, and how much had developed during the years he was with Mark.

I'll be there as soon as I can. I'll text you when I get there, then tell me where to meet you?

He responded, *Sure. See you soon.* After that was a smiling emoji.

I admittedly felt guilty for the excited flutter in my chest. Ahmed was stressed out and losing his mind over this painting and the game he apparently couldn't find. This wasn't some golden opportunity for me to spend time with him.

But what could I say?

There were worse things than the prospect of spending an evening wandering around a carnival—even a fucking weird one—with Ahmed.

OKAY, weekday or not, there should've been a lot more traffic on the way into the carnival. The highway wasn't as busy as the interstate, but it did get a fair bit of use. And, like, there was a carnival. One that Ahmed had indicated in his texts wasn't exactly deserted right now. Where the fuck was everyone coming from if they weren't going through here? Were they all taking the long way?

No idea, but I wasn't going to look a gift horse in the mouth. I especially wasn't going to question anything when I pulled into the packed parking lot and the attendant directed me to a space that had just opened up near the front. In no time, I had a ticket and was on my way in.

A text from Ahmed directed me to a picnic area near a cluster of concession stands. Tables and benches were laid out in wobbly rows, and people ate corndogs, burgers, fries, elephant ears, funnel cakes—all the usual carnival fare.

And right there, scrolling his phone at a table near the scone vendor, was Ahmed.

I was glad he wasn't looking right then, because I damn near stumbled. Heat rushed into my cheeks and I rolled my eyes at my own stupidity.

Dude, you see this guy every damn day at work. Get a grip.

But right then, he looked up at me, and the warm early evening sun hit his olive skin and disarming brown eyes just right, and I *did* stumble that time.

"Shit!"

Ahmed was immediately on his feet. "Oh, God. Are you okay?"

"I'm fine! I'm fine!" I laughed and put up my hands as I regained my balance. "Apparently I need to watch where I'm going, though."

He looked worried for a second, but then he smirked, and as he reclaimed his seat, he said, "Yeah, be careful. Don't need *you* breaking an axle."

"Oh, you're so funny." I couldn't keep from chuckling. As I joined him at the table, I turned serious again. "Have you had any luck?"

He blew out a breath and shook his head. Gazing around, he said, "I swear it feels like this whole place is punking me. Like they just want to see how long I'll keep looking for the stupid game before I go crazy." He faced me again. "That would explain why people who are leading me to it keep disappearing, right? They're all fucking with me?"

"I guess it would? But why would they zero in on you?"

"Who says they are?" He shrugged and seemed to be warming up to the idea. "Maybe I'm not the only one. Or maybe they just randomly pick people to pass the time." Then he frowned. "Except with all the weird shit happening with this painting…"

"Hmm. Good point." I tapped the table. "Listen, why don't we grab something to eat, and then we'll go walk around and find it?" I studied him. "When was the last time you ate?"

"Uh." He chewed his lip. "I'm not sure. I grabbed a milkshake earlier, but I kind of lost track of time while I was walking around."

"How about some actual food, then? It'll clear your head. And I need to eat before I gnaw off my arm."

Ahmed was suddenly bolt upright. "Oh, shit. Did you skip dinner to come all the way out here? God, Jason, I'm sorry. I didn't want to keep you from—"

"Hey. Hey." I touched his forearm. "Relax. I said we'd do dinner, right? I grabbed a protein bar at work to keep me on my feet. Don't worry."

Oh, he worried. He always did. It was in his nature to worry about everyone, and he especially mother-henned those of us he cared about.

"Come on." I got up. "Let's eat."

Ahmed started to do the same but hesitated, looking around the picnic area. Settling back on the bench, he said, "Why don't you grab your food while I hold on to the table? Then I'll go get something."

I considered it. "Counteroffer—why don't you guard the table, and I'll get food for both of us? What sounds good?"

An adorable smile flickered across his lips. Then he bit his lip and glanced around again before meeting my gaze and shrugging. "You know what I like. I'll have whatever you're having." He reached for his wallet. "Here, let me cover it."

"Ahmed, I can—"

"Don't argue with me." He pulled out a couple of twenties and offered them to me. "You came all the way out here to deal with my irrational ass. Buying you dinner is the *least* I can do."

Well, if I knew one thing about Ahmed, it was when there was no point in trying to change his mind, and this was one of those times. He hated making people feel put upon, and if paying for my dinner meant he could be less hard on himself for asking me to come out here, then…fine.

"All right." I took the cash. "Back in a minute."

He nodded and gave me another smile. As I walked away from the table, I wondered if he knew what his smiles did to me. How easily he could derail my train of thought with just a look.

Then sadness tugged at me. No, he probably didn't know that. Because he'd spent the last God knew how long with someone who didn't appreciate anything about him.

As I moved from one concession stand to the next in search of food, I had to wonder if Mark had even *liked* Ahmed. He'd never seemed particularly happy when they were together, though to be fair, my only exposure to him was when I was around, and he definitely didn't like me. But what about when they were alone? It was difficult to picture them being cute and affectionate. I struggled to imagine Mark doing little things to make Ahmed happy.

That wasn't just my inability to see Mark as a decent boyfriend, either. More than once when a colleague received something from a partner—flowers, a note in their lunch, a sweet text message—I'd found myself envying them…and I'd caught a look on Ahmed's face that suggested he felt the same.

What was the point of being with someone who left you craving even the smallest token or gesture of affection?

I tried to shake off those thoughts as I got in line for one of the burger stands. Mark was gone. No point in fixating on him.

Though I could probably get away with silently enjoying his absence.

Good riddance, doucheweasel.

With Mark out of the picture, I wondered if Ahmed could be coaxed into joining our group of friends more often. He'd seemed interested whenever Lucas and I talked about going to the various climbing gyms in town. Peyton, Derek, and I definitely wouldn't say no if he wanted to come snowboarding with us. Mark had turned up his nose at kayaking for whatever reason, but maybe Ahmed would be game to give it a try; he'd loved the photos I'd posted after a trip last year.

Well, all I could do was try. Invite him along. See what piqued his interest. Try like hell to hide how giddy I was just imagining doing some of my favorite things in the world *with him.*

The concession line moved quickly, and when I reached the front, I ordered for both of us. In no time, I was balancing two baskets of burgers and fries in one hand and a drink holder with two sodas in the other. By some miracle, despite people moving around me in all directions, I made it back to the table without spilling a drop.

As soon as Ahmed saw me, he jumped up and took the drinks. "Good God, I'd have dropped this all over the place."

"Pfft. You're more coordinated than I am." I was grateful for the help, though, and with my hand now freed up, I could separate our food. "Okay, this one is…" I peered at the burger, then the fries. "Looks like it's mine, but they mixed up the sauce cups." I put the baskets down, then swapped the paper cups of dipping sauce. I liked barbecue sauce and ranch (not mixed together), and he preferred ketchup and mustard (usually mixed together).

Ahmed slid his burger closer, and his eyes lit up. "Ooh, they had swiss? Nice!"

"Yep. I also asked them to hold the onions on yours, but they were pretty busy, so check."

He lifted the bun, then put it back down. "No onions." Gazing at me across the table, he graced me with one of those adorable smiles. "Thank you for remembering that."

Something told me certain *other* people in his life hadn't bothered, but I left it alone. I just returned the smile, and we started eating.

"Oh my God," he murmured after one bite of his burger. "This is so fucking good."

"Right? I kind of thought they'd be like carnival food usually is—smells great, but tastes like tire tread."

He laughed as he reached for his drink. "I gotta say, I've been pleasantly surprised by everything I've eaten here."

"Same." Which was true, but this burger was *spectacular*. Perfectly cooked. Just the right amount of every condiment and topping. The lettuce and tomatoes were crisper than they had any right to be. Carnival burgers weren't *supposed* to be this good. I was pretty sure that was one of the laws of physics or something.

And the fries were exactly as good as they'd been the other night despite coming from a different vendor. Instead of getting an entire fry basket full, we each had what amounted to a handful arranged beside our burgers, and every one of them—every last one—was perfectly cooked and salted. Ahmed had poured the ketchup and mustard onto the paper in the basket so he could swirl some of it together, but he'd eaten a few fries without anything on them. That spoke volumes, since Ahmed had once declared that fries and chicken tenders were little more than vessels for sauces.

So yeah. Damn good fries and amazing burgers.

Somehow it all tasted even better than the other night. Maybe because I was hungry? It had been hours since lunch, after all, and that had been a disappointing sandwich chased by a mediocre cup of coffee.

Or, I mused as I ate a ranch-dipped fry, it could've been because I was relaxed and not walking on eggshells. I wasn't listening to someone bitch about every goddamned thing imaginable, though even Mark, despite what I suspected were his best efforts, hadn't been able to find a reason to complain about the food.

Which might have explained why Ahmed seemed to be relaxed and happily enjoying his dinner, too. Even with the reason he'd come here today in the first place, he wasn't wound nearly as tight as he'd been the other night.

It said a lot when trying to get rid of a legitimately cursed carnival prize was less stressful than spending an evening out with your boyfriend.

I dragged a fry through some barbecue sauce, but didn't get any farther with it than that. "Listen, um...aside from the picture and everything else going on...you did just break up with someone." I studied him and cautiously asked, "How are you doing with that?"

Ahmed sighed, staring at his food. "I haven't had much time to think about it, to be honest. It's been chaos from all directions ever since that night."

"It really has." I ate the fry I'd been holding.

Ahmed chewed thoughtfully on a bite of his burger, his expression distant. I was curious what was on his mind, but I didn't press. Then he looked at me. "Is it bad that I'm more relieved than anything now that Mark is gone?"

I jumped like he'd kicked me under the table, and I tried to keep my tone and expression casual. "Are you?"

His brow furrowed and his eyes lost focus. After a few

seconds, he nodded slowly. "I am. It's…" He blew out a breath and slouched over his elbows on the picnic table. "I was really upset when he left, but now that he's gone, it's…" He absently ran another fry through the yellow-streaked orange mixture of ketchup and mustard. "Honestly? It's like a huge weight off my shoulders."

"Yeah?"

Ahmed nodded slowly. Grimacing, he asked, "Is that wrong?"

I took a good thirty seconds to think about how to respond to that. Finally, I asked, "Do you want my honest answer?"

His eyebrow flicked up. "Well, now I definitely do." Studying me curiously, he popped the fry into his mouth and chewed as he waited for me to respond.

I gnawed the inside of my cheek, trying to figure out exactly how to say what I was thinking. And how much of it.

He deserved honesty, though. That, and if he'd been quietly miserable with Mark, maybe he needed to know that someone else had seen it, too.

Finally, I took a deep breath. "I think you *should* be relieved that he's gone. Mark's a dick."

Ahmed blinked.

I pulled another fry off the pile and stabbed it into the barbecue sauce. "He treated you like shit, at least whenever I was around. And…I don't know." I shrugged. "You just always seemed happier away from him."

"I did?"

I nodded. "I think the most relaxed I've ever seen you was when he was in New York for a couple of weeks last year."

Ahmed's eyes lost focus again, as if he were rewinding that period. Mark had gone to some training thing for his job, and Ahmed had been like a different person the whole time. Instead of being sad that he was alone for a while, he was… Well, it was kind of like when Kim's parents had taken her twin toddlers for a weekend. She loved them dearly, but the break had rejuvenated her. I knew some parents who felt guilty for wanting a break from their kids, but I got it, especially when they were little—it didn't mean they didn't love their kids. Just meant kids were a lot of work.

Partners…weren't supposed to be as much work as toddlers or teenagers. They were supposed to be teammates. They were supposed to help shoulder a person's burdens, not add to them.

After a while, Ahmed exhaled. He started to speak. Hesitated.

Then he checked his phone and cleared his throat. "We should probably get moving if we're going to find that booth." He motioned at our surroundings. "I have no idea how late they stay open on weeknights."

I recognized a subject change when I saw it, and I didn't press even as a ball of lead formed in my stomach. He was probably still sorting through a lot of complicated feelings about his relationship, and talking about it wasn't easy.

I was just scared I'd stepped over a line. Mark *was* a dick. Ahmed *did* deserve better.

But maybe it hadn't been the right time—or my place at all—to tell him that.

What the hell was I supposed to say now?

CHAPTER 10

Ahmed

The burger and fries had been perfect. Hell, even the soda had stayed fizzy all the way to the end, and despite the lingering heat of the day, the ice didn't melt and water down the flavor. I swore every drink I ever had at the county fair was flat and gross by halfway through. Not here. That had to be sorcery or something, but whatever. I had no complaints.

Still, as Jason and I walked the carnival, that amazing meal sat heavy in my stomach. I didn't think I'd eaten too much or that it had anything to do with the food. No, it was the conversation we'd had over dinner.

Jason wasn't usually the type to be blunt. In fact, out of all of us at the clinic, he was the one who struggled the most with delivering difficult news. He could do it—the job required it—but it was harder for him than the rest of us. Which said something, because that part of the job sucked for everyone. Fortunately it was the doctors who usually issued the heaviest news, but sometimes we had to gently explain things that were difficult to hear, and that was never fun.

Jason always took it hard, and he always worried himself sick afterward that he could have approached it better, or said it more tactfully, or something. He had nothing to worry about in that department—no one would ever accuse him of being tactless or too blunt.

So what he'd said about Mark had me seriously off-balance. Maybe even more than this whole cursed painting debacle.

How bad did Mark have to be—and how obvious—for *Jason* to come right out and say that he was a dick?

And how clueless did I have to be to miss it?

Except…

I hadn't missed it. Maybe I hadn't *consciously* realized it, but it was there. These past several days, I'd marveled at what it was like to no longer feel the weight of being under Mark's thumb, which had made me think back on our five years together and see just how far under it I'd been.

I couldn't remember being happy with Mark. I couldn't remember being excited to introduce him to my friends or my family. There had to have been a time when things were good between us, but I…couldn't remember. I was vaguely aware of some distant, faded memories, but they were so far back, I couldn't bring them into focus.

Because I'd been fucking miserable.

Halfway down a row of games, in the gap between the crowds waiting to throw darts at balloons or shoot squirt guns at targets to win a plastic horse race, I halted abruptly. Jason did too, and when he turned to me, there was concern instead of annoyance written all over his face. All *Is everything okay?* without a trace of *What the fuck is your problem?* or *Jesus, what now?*

"You're right. What you said—about Mark being a dick.

You're…" I let my shoulders slump under the invisible weight I was tired of carrying. "You're right."

Obviously I'd been with Mark for way too long, because I fully expected an *"I told you so,"* even though that would be wildly out of character for Jason.

Instead, I got exactly what anyone who knew Jason would expect from him: a sympathetic look and a soft, "I'm sorry. You deserved better than that."

I ran my hand through my hair. "I can't believe I put up with him for so fucking long. How was I so damn stupid?"

"You're not stupid," Jason said softly. "It's always easier to see things like that from the outside." He paused. "You know, like all that guidance we get for spotting patients who are dealing with domestic violence?"

I blinked. "Mark never laid a hand on me."

"No, but he treated you like shit." Jason's features tightened as if this conversation were physically painful for him. "How many patients have we had who insisted everything was fine, and then later, we realized it wasn't?" He shrugged subtly. "Some of them were beaten down so far, they really didn't think there was anything wrong. And I think Mark had the effect on you. Even if he never touched you, he had you beaten down all the same."

It was suddenly hard to swallow. I couldn't look at Jason, so I stared at the popcorn-littered dirt at our feet as the carnival went on around us and the last half-decade of my life flashed through my mind. I wanted to argue with him, if only to insist I wasn't as stupid and oblivious as I felt. But I really couldn't. And now that I thought about it, I'd asked myself more than once throughout our relationship if he was mistreating me, and then I'd remember those patients I saw who were really being abused, and I'd shut down that train of thought.

"He's just in a pissy mood and being snappy," I'd tell myself. *"It isn't like he just shoved you down a flight of stairs or—"*

But that didn't matter. He was being an asshole. Whether it fit one person or another's definition of abuse—whether it even fit my definition—didn't matter, because his behavior didn't fit any reasonable definition of how to treat a partner.

And I put up with that for five years?

Jason's hands landed gently on my shoulders. "Ahmed. Look at me."

Shame and embarrassment wanted me to keep my gaze fixed on the ground, but I did as I was told. I was both surprised and not to see nothing but gentle empathy in his eyes.

"You can't go back and change any of it," he said evenly. "And you definitely can't blame yourself because he was an insufferable jerkwad who didn't deserve the time of day from you."

The vehemence startled me.

He went on, "The important thing is that he's gone. Now you can actually live your life again, and not worry about keeping him happy."

I slowly released my breath, wondering if he knew how much I'd needed to hear that, not to mention how much the weight of his hands on my shoulders reassured me. "You're right. I know. It's just hard to process, I guess."

"I'm sure it is." He squeezed my shoulders, then let go, and I had to literally bite my tongue to stop myself from saying, *"Put them back."* What the hell was *that* all about?

God, I was a mess. Probably a side effect of everything in my world getting turned on its ass lately.

I glanced around, our brightly lit and festive surroundings coming into focus. Had I really come out here and spent hours searching for a stupid game just to get rid of this damn prize? Hell, the painting probably wasn't even cursed. Mark was the curse that had been on my life for half a fucking decade, and he was gone now.

"You know what? Let's…" I looked at Jason again. "Let's just get hell out of here. If we haven't found that game yet, we're probably not going to."

His forehead creased. "What about the picture?"

Instead of answering, I brought my bag around from my back, unzipped it, and withdrew the soot-dusted painting. I found a nearby trashcan and tossed the damn thing in, letting it fall into a nest of empty cups and some half-eaten nachos.

"There." I zipped my bag again. "Now it's gone."

He seemed uncertain for a second, but then he grinned. "Perfect. Now let's hope it stays gone."

"Right?" I laughed, and we started heading toward the carnival's exit. "Thanks again for coming up here. Maybe I needed the sanity check more than the help finding the button game."

Jason shrugged, offering me a smile that almost made me trip over my own feet. "Any time. I'm glad you're feeling better about it."

So was I. If anything, I was a little disappointed this weird day and evening were coming to a close. I couldn't ask him to stay out here, though. We did have to work tomorrow, after all.

As we left the carnival and headed into the sprawling field of parked cars, that disappointment dug a little deeper. I really didn't want this evening to be over, but hell if I could come up with a reason to keep it going.

Then Jason stopped, though not quite as suddenly as I had earlier. He slowed down, and as I did the same, he came to a gentle halt. Turning to me, his expression unusually (and maybe just a little bit adorably) shy, he said, "You know, I could go for something sweet after that dinner." The shyness intensified. "Want to grab some pie at the trucker café?"

I couldn't explain it, but the prospect of sitting down in that old, dusty café with Jason for a late-night piece of pie was…amazing. And not just because their pie was awesome. It was also an excuse not to call it a night too soon, so I said, "Sure. See you in fifteen or so?"

"Yeah." He smiled. "I'll see you there."

THE CAFÉ HAD ABOUT twenty different pie flavors, but they weren't all available every day. It was kind of a crapshoot if you wanted something specific—especially as the day went on, the odds of your favorite running out went up—but I always found something here that sounded good.

Tonight, the remaining options were cherry, peach, pecan, Key lime, and strawberry rhubarb. I opted for peach while Jason picked cherry, and we both asked for them warm and with ice cream. We were barely two sips into our coffee —this place had the best coffee, oh my God—when our server returned with the pie.

Jason took a bite and made a happy sound. "I swear." He pointed at his slice with his fork. "If they opened up a booth at that carnival, they'd make millions."

"Right? Man, these are good."

We ate in silence for a few minutes. It was hard not to— their pies were seriously divine, and they needed to be enjoyed, not just absentmindedly nibbled. Lucas and Tina were hardcore foodies, and they'd both turned up their noses the first time we'd come here, but they were believers now.

When we were about halfway through our desserts, Jason met my gaze across the table. "So, um. I don't want to dwell on Mark." He gestured dismissively with his fork. "I'm sure he's the last thing you want to talk about."

I nodded in agreement. I was more than happy to not talk about him again for a long, long time.

"I am curious, though…" Jason picked up a cherry on his fork and ran it through some of the melted ice cream. "Now that he's out of the picture, what kinds of things do you want to do?"

I cocked my head. "What do you mean?"

"Well, you know how it is. Even with good relationships that end amicably, there's always something we give up. Like when you date someone who doesn't like some kind of food that you do." He quirked his lips as if he were trying to think of another example. "Or like when my sister really wanted to get a cat, but her boyfriend was allergic. He was a perfectly nice guy, and things ended fine—they're still friends to this day—but the minute he moved out, she went to the shelter and adopted a pair of cats." He shrugged. "It wasn't a vindictive thing or like a fuck-you. It was just something she could do now, and it helped her move on."

"Oh. Huh." I poked at a piece of peach. "I…hadn't given it any thought."

"I don't doubt it." He laughed softly. "You've been, uh, kind of preoccupied."

With a dry chuckle, I nodded. "No shit." As I skewered the peach, I met his gaze. "Tell me some things you did after breakups."

"Me? Uh…" He shifted in his chair, some color blooming in his cheeks the way it always did when he was put on the spot.

Oh my God, he was cute.

I tamped down that thought and took a bite of my pie while I waited for him to answer.

"I haven't really had that many relationships, so there isn't

—Oh! I remember one." He took a quick sip of coffee. "It must be, I don't know, seven or eight years ago at least, since we dated while I was in nursing school. He wanted to go to grad school in California, and neither of us wanted to do the long-distance thing, so..." He trailed off into a shrug.

I nodded. "Makes sense. Long-distance is tough."

"Especially when you're both broke college kids." He grimaced.

"Ugh, I don't miss those days."

"Neither do I. Anyway..." He idly picked at his pie, and he chuckled quietly before he went on. "He was vegan. And he really couldn't deal with meat. Like the smell of it, even the sight of it, bothered him. He wasn't crazy about people eating dairy or eggs around him, either, but it didn't bother him the way meat did. So we kind of had this compromise where I wouldn't order meat when we went out, but he didn't mind if I got dairy."

"Let me guess." I grinned. "First night on your own, you went out for steak."

Jason's laugh lit up everything—including every nerve ending in my body—and the sheepish way he shrugged and blushed was far more endearing than it should've been. Oblivious to my brain short-circuiting, he said, "Well, I was a broke college student, so it was actually a Philly cheesesteak. But same principle."

"And I'll bet you enjoyed the hell out of it, didn't you?"

"I..." The smile fell a little, and he turned thoughtful. "I mean, I did? It was amazing. Not as good as what we had tonight, but seriously good. And it...I guess it was bitter-sweet. It was nice to be able to order whatever I wanted, but it kind of drove home that we were done."

"Oh. Yeah, that would be some mixed feelings, wouldn't it?"

"It was. Mostly good, though. I think if we'd had a nasty

breakup, it would've been a lot more satisfying. Like a fuck-you, you know?"

I nodded. "I get that."

"So, is there anything like that in life after Mark?" he asked. "Something you've wanted to do that you haven't been able to?"

We continued eating as I considered it. Maybe I shouldn't have been surprised by the rush of possibilities that crashed through my mind. It wasn't fun and rebellious things like eating a forbidden meal or adopting a cat. No, it was the realization that if I was halfway to work and suddenly couldn't remember if I'd thoroughly cleaned the sink after I'd trimmed my beard, I wouldn't have to either turn around or spend the whole day worrying about it. I wouldn't have to strategize when to leave and which route to take home so I could get there before Mark and make sure I hadn't left an errant whisker. I could count the number of times I'd actually forgotten on one hand with fingers to spare, but the reaction had been enough to make me sure from then on that *this time*, I'd *definitely* forgotten.

I could save up episodes of a show until I was in the right headspace to watch them. No more choosing between listening to Mark bitch because he wanted to watch it or gritting my teeth through it when I was too emotionally wrung out from a long day at the clinic.

I could come home from one of those long days and just quietly decompress without having to wear myself out by insisting I wasn't ignoring him or cold-shouldering him.

I could hang out with my friends without that constant worry over what he'd go off about once we were finally alone. I could hang out with them without him at all. When they asked me to join them snowboarding or climbing—and they always did even though we all knew I'd say no—I could finally say yes.

My answer to Jason's question came tumbling out in a single word: "Breathe."

Jason's eyes widened. "What?"

"I can..." I paused to collect my thoughts. "I can breathe."

He stared at me, his expression encouraging me to elaborate but somehow reassuring me that I didn't have to. What a concept—someone who didn't demand I spell out every thought that ran across my mind or emotion that rolled across my face.

I thumbed the edge of my pie plate. "Mark was just... impossible to please. Everything was his way or the highway, and..." I laughed bitterly and reached for my coffee. "Should've picked the highway a long, long time ago."

Jason watched me, but he didn't ask why I'd stayed instead of bailing. His soft expression again invited me to go on if I wanted to, but he still wasn't pushy about it.

I took another bite of pie as I thought about how to continue. After a sip of coffee, I said, "You know how some days at the clinic just drain you?"

"Oh, I know." Jason picked up his own coffee. "I'll take it over working in the E.D. any day of the week, but there are some days..." He whistled and shook his head.

"Right? So I'll get home sometimes and just want to chill. Watch something stupid on TV that I've seen five hundred times."

He nodded. "I am very familiar with the post-work cartoon binge."

A relieved laugh burst out of me, and I wasn't even sure why. Validation, maybe? I didn't know. "Yes. Exactly." Humor fading, I leaned back in my chair. "I also like some of the heavier shows, you know? The dramas and stuff. But after a really rough day..."

Jason grimaced sympathetically and nodded again. "I get that. Either my head's too tired to keep up with what's going on, or I'm just too emotionally done to deal with whatever happens."

"Seriously. It's… Ugh, I watched one of our shows after a day like that, and they killed off one of my favorite characters. That was too much, you know?"

"Oh God, yeah. That's why I stick with the cartoons, especially the ones I've seen a hundred times. Why would you watch something like that on—" His teeth snapped shut, and his eyes widened, then softened with more sympathy. "He insisted on watching it, didn't he?"

I nodded. "He hated getting behind on any of our shows. I could sometimes get away with putting off one episode, but if we ended up more than two behind, he'd be insufferable until we watched them."

Jason inclined his head. "I'm tempted to ask if he understood how taxing your job can be, but I feel like I already know the answer."

A week or two ago, I wouldn't have been able to connect the dots. Free from Mark's constant oppressive presence, I landed on the answer almost immediately: "He didn't care."

Jason nodded slowly. "That's kind of what I gathered."

"Ugh." I stabbed an unsuspecting piece of peach and grumbled, "I can't believe I put up with that for so long, but it just became so…"

"Normal?" Jason offered.

"Yeah. That." I sighed. "Here's to a new normal after Mark."

Chuckling, Jason held up his coffee, and I managed a laugh myself as I clicked my cup against his.

We let the subject of Mark drop after that, which I appreciated. My mind kept whirring on the topic, though. Not because I was hung up on our breakup or anything—if he walked in right now and wanted to get back together, I'd send him packing without a second thought.

No, I was just caught on the fact that a lot of truths had made themselves known tonight. They all seemed to fall out of the clear blue sky, and at the same time were so obvious, I couldn't believe I'd never thought about them before.

Something in the back of my mind was trying desperately to connect Mark's reason for leaving with me sitting here right now with Jason. As if, just by talking over pie at this roadside café, I was confirming everything Mark had accused me of.

I shut that down, though. Mark was wrong about my friendship with Jason. Even if I suddenly fell in love with Jason right then and there at the café table, I hadn't been in love with him while I was with Mark.

Apparently that was how far Mark had gotten under my damn skin—even now that I was single, I was feeling guilty and ashamed for daring to have a spark of attraction to someone, especially the man he'd accused me of cheating with.

But I'm not attracted to Jason like that.

I stole a glance at him.

Am I?

I shook the thought away. That was something to sort out some other time. Not here. Not now. Not after I'd been through a psychological wringer today. And maybe not while I was sitting right across from Jason and wondering how I'd never noticed the little flecks of gold in his near-green hazel eyes.

We didn't stay much longer after that. We did have to work the next morning, after all, and we still had to drive home. I insisted on picking up the check—seemed like the least I could do—and we headed out into the steadily cooling night.

Behind his truck and my car, we paused and faced each other.

"Thank you again." I smiled up at him. "For coming out here to help me try to find that damn game. And just...you know. Hanging out."

He returned my smile. "Don't mention it. You know I'm always around if you need something. And you did buy dinner *and* dessert, so..."

I laughed and stepped closer to hug him, and as he wrapped his arms around me, I didn't question the flutter in my chest. Those weren't butterflies. This wasn't a crush or anything like that. Jason was my friend and my colleague. Period. I was just relieved to be free.

Jason released me, and as I drew back, our eyes met.

No butterflies. Right?

Just freedom?

He cleared his throat and broke eye contact, and even in the low light of the parking lot, he couldn't hide the blush. "I, um... Anyway. We should get going. I need to get some sleep, and Kim will be salty with me if I'm late tomorrow."

I laughed, breaking this weird spell, and I wasn't sure if I was disappointed or relieved by that. Something to think about on the drive home, I guess. "Yeah. I'm pretty sure Rachel will have my hide if I take another day."

"Eh." Jason shrugged. "She probably wishes you'd just take a vacation day like a normal person instead of waiting for an emergency to call out."

I chuckled. "Hmm, probably. She's been after me for a while to take some PTO." I straightened. "Hey, maybe *she* cursed me!"

"Mmhmm, maybe." He playfully nudged me. "So take some vacation time already."

"I will, I will. But not tomorrow." I gestured at our cars. "See you in the morning?"

"Yeah." That startlingly beautiful smile again. "See you in the morning."

We got into our respective vehicles and headed for home. As I followed Jason's taillights down the highway toward town, I had no idea what to think or feel about anything. My whole world had been weird ever since that first trip to the carnival, and it didn't feel any less weird right now.

Hopefully the bad luck would stop now that I'd taken the damn painting back to the carnival and left it there. Hopefully I could start diving into my new normal as a single man who didn't have to live on eggshells anymore. I still had a lot of things to think about—a lot of feelings to sort out—but hopefully things would, little by little, start to make sense.

Some things already did.

I was definitely relieved to be free of my ex.

And I was grateful beyond words for my friend.

CHAPTER 11

Jason

That night, I slept better than I had recently. Part of that was probably because I'd come home late after a long, busy day at work. That would've sucked the life out of anyone.

More than that, though, I was pretty sure it was just relief. I hadn't realized how much I'd been worrying about Ahmed lately until that worry lifted away and let me crash. Hopefully Ahmed had been sleeping better too; even with all the chaos going on in his world, just getting away from that jackwagon had to be a relief. Getting rid of the cursed painting probably helped, too.

I'd check in with him at work. See how he was after last night.

First things first—getting my butt to work. After a shower, I dressed, put some coffee into a travel mug, and left. Traffic was light as always since I didn't live or work in a terribly busy part of the city. Once school was back in, there'd be the race to get ahead of the buses so I didn't get stuck behind one, but for now, the kids were still enjoying their summer break.

Lucky, I thought, and chuckled just because I was in a good mood.

I reached an intersection that turned from the two-lane road onto a four-lane arterial, and I waited at the light. When it turned green, I followed traffic around the righthand turn.

As I accelerated around the corner, though, the steering wheel wobbled in my hands, pulling hard to the right and nearly taking me off the road.

"Oh, don't you dare," I muttered. "Come on. Not..."

But there was no mistaking that insistent pull. It was one of those things that felt bizarre as hell the first time, but was instantly recognizable any time after that.

Swearing, I nosed off onto the shoulder, which took some extra effort since, even as it pulled to that side, the truck really didn't want to be steered. I managed, though, getting safely over the white line. I watched in the side mirror until I had enough room to get out, then swung open the door, hopped down, and went around to the other side.

And there it was—my front passenger tire, flat as a pancake.

"Seriously?" I demanded of my truck. "Are you fucking kidding me?"

The truck, being an inanimate object, didn't respond. The equally inanimate tire didn't inflate.

I rolled my eyes and quickly texted Rachel to let her know I had a flat and would be in late.

You ok? she wrote back. *Need any help?*

I'm good. It'll just take a few minutes to change it, then I'll be on the road again.

Ok. If you need to call AAA or something, let me know. We can cover you.

I appreciated that. I covered for my coworkers a lot when

they needed it, and everyone returned the favor when they could. So I wasn't worried about leaving anyone in a lurch or getting in trouble. I was just fucking annoyed because I was only halfway through my first cup of coffee, and now I had to change a goddamned tire.

I laughed to myself as I opened up the passenger door to get the tools out to change the tire. Ahmed was going to love this. After all the vehicle fuckery he'd had to deal with, now I had a flat. Maybe we should tell everyone at the clinic to take their cars in for tune-ups, just to be absolutely sure no one had any timebombs waiting to add to the chaos.

I had a bunch of crap stashed in the gap behind my seats, so it took a minute to shuffle all that around and get to the compartment behind the passenger seat. Once I'd done that, I unscrewed the knob, popped off the plastic cover, and—

Jumped back with a yelp, just barely stopping myself from stumbling ass-over-teakettle into the ditch.

"What the fuck?" I muttered over the sound of passing cars. Heart pounding, I stared at my truck as if it had a venomous snake curled behind the seats.

No way. Fucking impossible.

In fact...

No. No, I'd imagined it. Clearly I had. Because there was no way in hell...

In fact, now that I thought about it, I hadn't opened that hatch in a while. Maybe there was a manual or something in there that I'd forgotten about. That was it. That was all I'd seen. I'd just caught such a fleeting glance, I hadn't had time to really make sense of what I was seeing before my lizard brain started screaming, *"Danger! Run away!"*

I rolled my eyes at my own stupidity, marched back to my truck, and yanked that cover off again.

And it was still fucking there.

Plain as day.

Not a manual.

Not unless Ford had started printing their manuals with weird old-timey carousel designs on the covers.

In particular, the kind that perfectly matched the painting Ahmed had—right in front of my eyes—dumped into a trashcan last night. The same one we'd both watched burn to nothing in a video that no longer existed on either of our phones.

I couldn't even convince myself it wasn't the same painting. Not that that would've made much *more* sense, but there was still soot on the edges, splatter marks where Peyton's "potion" had landed, and on one side, a dried smear of what I thought was cheese sauce. It was, somehow, the same damn picture.

"What the fuck?" I whispered.

This wasn't possible. I'd watched Ahmed put it in the trash. The only time we were separated after that had been when we'd driven to the café, and even then, I'd been able to see his headlights the whole way. He'd been behind me on the way home, too.

Unless he'd waited until I turned into my apartment complex, whipped around, gone back to the carnival, fished it out of the trash, and come clear back to my apartment to play a prank on me...

Except he didn't have a key to my truck. And nothing I'd piled on top of the compartment had been disturbed. It was messy, yeah, but the kind of messy that was familiar—if something had moved, I'd have noticed.

He couldn't have put it there. And even if he could've, that wasn't Ahmed. He was too spooked by this damn thing to use it to play a prank. Even as committed as he could be to practical jokes, he wouldn't have put in *that* much time and effort.

And there was still the issue of the truck key. The clutter.

Plus the flat tire—no, that was definitely not an Ahmed

prank. No one who spent time working in an emergency department fucked around with causing cars to fail in ways that could result in crashes. Not unless they were complete psychopaths, and Ahmed was *not* a psychopath.

What the fuck?

Seriously, *what the fuck?*

I ended up having to call AAA after all because I was too shaken up to trust myself to safely change this tire. I had visions of the truck coming down on me because I'd screwed up with the jack, or a lug nut snapping off because the universe was having a ball at my expense. I didn't give a damn if anyone thought I was less of a man because I had to have someone come change my tire. Pride was the farthest thing from my mind right now.

In the end, I walked into to work around eleven.

"Oh, you made it!" Rachel stood up from her desk as I came in. "Were you able to get the tire replaced? Fixed?"

I shook my head. "No, it's… The tow truck dropped it off at the shop. They'll call me when it's ready to go."

She blinked. "Wow, you and Ahmed are both having the worst luck with tires lately."

I laughed, probably sounding like I was on the verge of hysteria. The shoe fit, after all. "Yeah, something like that. Speaking of—is he with a patient right now?"

"He's…" She peered at the real-time schedule on her screen. "He's with someone in three, but they should be wrapping up soon." Gesturing toward the desks in the back, she added, "We've got a bunch of people waiting, so as soon as you can, I need you to start taking patients."

I nodded. "Yeah. Yeah, will do."

I was shaky as I logged in. I debated bowing out of seeing patients until I had my head together, but there really wasn't a tactful way to tell my boss that I was freaking out because I'd found a cursed painting from a weird carnival in my truck while I was trying to fix a flat tire.

Fortunately, my training to become an RN had ensured I could function at close enough to one hundred percent to treat patients even when I was hungry, sleep-deprived, stressed-out, distracted, or—as I was discovering today— dealing with a cursed and cheese-encrusted picture of a creepy carousel.

It was a solid hour and a half of patients and charts before Ahmed and I crossed paths, and when we did, he did a double take.

"Hey." He came closer, worry all over his expression. "You okay? Rachel said you got a flat, but you look like..." He gestured at his own face. "That's not 'I got a flat tire.'"

"No, it isn't." I hesitated. "You have a minute?"

He checked the time and his iPad. "I'm actually about to take lunch. What do you need?"

I checked my own iPad. I didn't have much time, especially since I was working through lunch to make up for being late, but I could steal a couple of minutes. I nodded toward Ahmed's office. As we headed that way, I grabbed a manila envelope I'd left on my desk.

Shutting the door behind us, Ahmed regarded me worriedly. "What's going on? You okay?"

"When I went to change my tire, I found this in with the jack and tire iron." I held out the envelope.

He eyed it, and his spine slowly straightened. He drew back a little as if I'd offered him a spider. Though he couldn't have seen the contents of the envelope, the size didn't leave much to the imagination. Not for someone who'd been trying like hell to get rid of something that was roughly this size.

He met my gaze. "That's not funny, Jason."

"No, it isn't." I opened the flap and slid the painting free, and as the color drained from Ahmed's face, I said, "I don't know how to explain it. But I swear to God, it was there. I have no idea how it got there, and it damn near gave me a heart attack."

Ahmed swallowed hard, staring warily at the painting in my hand. "There's no way. That's just... It's not possible. I..." He raked his fingers through his hair and swore. "*How?*"

I shook my head slowly. "No idea. But...dude, if I wasn't spooked before..."

"I know, right?" He shivered, then blew out a breath. "Okay, we *have* to take it back to that game. Obviously leaving it at the carnival isn't enough. We need to find that guy, shove this thing back into his hands, and...I don't know." He flailed his arms. "Say an incantation or throw salt over our shoulders or... whatever the hell people do when they think something is cursed."

I nodded. "Think the potion lady has anything that'll..." I trailed off, because oh my God, I sounded insane. But Ahmed was nodding because we were both probably losing our minds at this point. Here we were, completely rational trained medical professionals, talking in all seriousness about curses and potions and all that ridiculousness.

On the other hand, no amount of medical training or healthy skepticism did much to explain a progressively dirtier painting that kept reappearing in places it had no business being.

Ahmed chafed his arms. "Ugh. I'm so done with this. I swear, I'm going to ask someone to show me where the booth is, and then I'm going to handcuff myself to them so I don't lose them in the damn crowd this time."

Twenty-four hours ago, I probably would've laughed at that and said it couldn't be *that* bad. After this morning, I wondered if we could do same-day Amazon Prime for a set of handcuffs. I didn't even care if that made me irrational. There was nothing rational about this situation, so...fuck it.

I didn't actually order them, but driving back out to that godforsaken field to get rid of this thing once and for all? Fuck yes. "So...carnival tonight?"

"Definitely." Ahmed nodded sharply. "After work?"

"I'll drive."

CHAPTER 12

Ahmed

*W*e still couldn't find that stupid game.

I swore we'd covered every last inch of this godforsaken carnival, to the point we were starting to recognize the faces of everyone who worked here. Three different people led us toward the booth, only to get waylaid or lost in the crowd, including the girl at the dart toss booth who I'd talked to the first time.

"Everything all starts to look the same after a while," she'd chirped as she led us away from her booth down the crowded fairway. "Trust me, you'll walk right by something fifty times and never see it until you trip over it. That game is right down—"

"Michelle!" an urgent voice broke through the noise, causing our guide to stop dead and whirl on her heel. "Oh, thank God!" An older gentleman jogged up next to us. "Pete's got his hand stuck in the Wheel of Fortune, and you're the best at getting people out of it."

Then he had her by the hand and was half-leading, half-dragging her in another direction.

She glanced back at us, gesturing in the direction we'd been going, and then…

She was gone.

"What the…" I turned in a slow circle, scanning our surroundings, before directing a plaintive and semi-panicked look on Jason. "I didn't imagine it, right? She was here, and then…" I waved my hand.

"Not unless we're both hallucinating the same thing," he said. "Fucking weird."

I exhaled, my shoulders sagging. The backpack strap suddenly seemed even heavier, biting into my tired muscles as if I were carrying bricks instead of that thin picture that wasn't quite the size of a piece of printer paper. "We're never going to get rid of this thing."

Jason pursed his lips, absently thumbing the edge of his jaw. "You know, that thing she said…about walking by something fifty times and then tripping over it? Maybe she's right."

"How so?"

He shrugged. "It's like every time we've needed an ATM. I never actually see them—or at least never notice them—until I'm looking for one. Then it's always…" He glanced around before gesturing past me. "Right over there."

I followed where he'd indicated. We had walked past that game—the one where you tossed ping pong balls into fishbowls in hopes of winning a goldfish—a hundred times, and I'd never noticed the ATM tucked in right next to it. Christ, with as many ATMs as this place seemed to have, and how the chunky beige machines clashed with the dark stained wood and colorful lights, it was kind of amazing we weren't tripping over them all the time.

I turned to Jason again. "But when we go looking for an

ATM, we find one even though we never see them until we're actually looking. This is the opposite—we found the button game just strolling around. Now that we're looking…" I flailed a hand at our surroundings.

"Right," he said. "So maybe this is the reverse. Like when you're trying to find the remote, then you give up and stop looking, and it magically appears on the coffee table."

I chewed my lip. "Okay, I guess that makes as much sense as anything. So what do you suggest?

"Maybe we need to go back to what we did before—just walk around. Play games. Eat food. Ride rides." He shrugged. "We'll probably stumble right into it when we stop actually looking for it."

I thought about it. Logically, it didn't make any sense. With as many times as we'd been around this damn carnival, we should've seen that stupid game by now. On the other hand, what did we have to lose by giving it a try? A warm evening of wandering around a carnival together without my now-ex-boyfriend's attitude putting a damper on everything?

In an instant, I was onboard. "Okay." I smiled. "Let's do it. Just enjoy the carnival and see what happens."

He smiled back, and… God, no wonder I couldn't find anything. How was I supposed to look at anything but him?

What the hell?

I shook that away, and we started wandering.

"Want to try that game?" He nodded toward the one with the fishbowls. "You can probably win a goldfish that's possessed by Satan."

I snorted. "They're probably all telekinetic."

"How do you figure?"

I stopped and pointed at a teenage boy who tried unsuccessfully to land a ball in one of the colorful bowls. "Because they use their powers to divert the balls in or out of a bowl, depending on whether they want to go home with that particular person."

"Ooh, so they're telekinetic *and* judgy as fuck." Jason whistled. "Now I kind of want one of the little assholes."

"We could totally bring it to the office. Make all the pharma reps say hello to it, and if something flies off the desk, then we'd know that rep was shady as hell."

Jason laughed, unaware of what that was doing to my body temperature. "Considering some of the reps we get in there, wouldn't that just make a gigantic mess?"

"Well, yeah." I shrugged. "But it would be worth it."

"Hmm, true. It would be funny as hell."

The boy who was trying to win eventually gave up. That, or he'd run out of money—at a dollar a ticket and a ticket per throw, it added up. Beside him, a little girl had convinced her dad to buy her a single throw. The dad crouched beside her and seemed to give her some pointers for how to hold the ball and toss it, and she nodded solemnly as if absorbing everything he said.

Finally, he stood and told her, "Go ahead."

She looked at him. The bowls. The ball.

Then she hucked that ball without any regard for her dad's instructions about form or strategy, and it bounced wildly off the rim of one bowl...

Off a decorative sign...

Banking off a post at an impossible angle...

And right into one of the fishbowls with a tiny but satisfying splash.

The girl cheered like she'd just scored a Super Bowl touchdown. Her dad's jaw fell open. The teenage boy huffed about "stupid rigged games" and stomped off.

The woman running the booth just smiled and asked the girl a question I didn't hear.

"Wait, wait, wait," Jason whispered, "I thought you were bullshitting about them being telekinetic and judgy!"

"I was!"

"Okay, but..." He flailed his hand toward the game. "Tell me that wasn't the work of a telekinetic goldfish!"

The outburst was probably louder than he'd intended it, and it attracted a few odd looks from people around us, including the father whose daughter had probably just won a haunted fish.

The woman behind the counter handed the girl her new pet, looked right at us, and offered us an odd but vaguely creepy smile.

Jason and I looked at each other, and my face had to be full of as much WTF as his was in that moment.

"Uh." He swallowed. "Keep walking?"

"Keep walking."

We kept walking.

At the end of the row of games, the caricaturist came into view, and renewed sadness started chipping away at me. I slowed, gazing at the artist, who was currently drawing a pair of giggling teenagers who wouldn't sit still.

"What's wrong?" Jason asked.

I nodded toward the artist. "The whole getting-drawn thing. It was... It should've been a lot more fun than it was, you know?"

He studied me but quickly seemed to connect the dots. "Mark."

Sighing, I nodded again. "Yeah. And I can't even enjoy the picture because he's in it." I groaned. "Because Mark was *everywhere* I was for the last five years."

"He really was clingy, wasn't he?" Jason sounded cautious. "Seemed like the only place you ever went without him was work."

My shoulders sagged. "That's about right, yeah. God, I wish I could Photoshop him out of my life."

"Wouldn't that be nice?" Then Jason pointed at the caricaturist. "As long as we're here, you want to get another one? Like, one that doesn't have that cranky jackass in it."

A laugh burst out of me. "You really didn't like him, did you?"

"I…" He chewed his lip. "Not really, no."

I didn't press, instead shifting the topic back to the artist. "So you really want to do one together? Just you and me?"

Jason smirked. "Well, unless you want to grab some random stranger to join us…yes?"

I laughed. "Okay, not a random stranger. But us—hell, why not?" I shrugged as if his suggestion hadn't just made the whole world tilt beneath my feet. "We could put it up at work."

"Now you're thinking. Let's do it."

We waited until the artist had finished with the people in front of us. While they guffawed and scoffed over his portrayal, we ponied up the money and sat down.

As he'd done the other night, the caricaturist studied both of us for a long moment.

Jason bumped his shoulder against mine and asked in a stage whisper, "Do I have anything in my teeth?" Then he flashed a ridiculously huge, toothy grin.

I snorted. "Oh my God. He's going to draw your dumb ass as a llama."

The artist actually chuckled at that.

Jason shrugged unrepentantly. "Hey, as long as there's nothing in my teeth."

"There could be," the artist suggested slyly.

Jason stilled. "Like what?"

"Don't know." A devilish grin came from behind the easel. "Perhaps we'll see."

"Aw, fuck." Jason turned to me and, in another loud whisper, he said, "He's going to draw me eating pizza with mushrooms on it, I just know it."

I burst out laughing. Jason could make the most hilariously disgusted faces when someone suggested putting mushrooms on pizza—something we all did when we ordered pizza at the clinic, just to fuck with him. Those expressions exaggerated in a cartoon would be the funniest thing ever. They had to be.

"He should!" I said through my laughter. "A big piece of deep-dish pizza with extra mushrooms and—"

"Oh *God*." Jason gagged and doubled over, making one of those faces. "Fuck. That's just wrong!"

"Wrong? They're just mushrooms!"

"They're an abomination that are unfit for human consumption!" He made another hilarious face, a mix of disgust and being horribly offended. "And people put them on pizza."

I was almost crying now, same as always when Jason all but dry-heaved over mushrooms on pizza. Elbowing him, I managed, "Oh my God, stop it. How's he supposed to draw me when I'm laughing this hard?"

"What?" Jason asked innocently. "It isn't like he's taking a photo. It won't blur if you move."

"Not unless you want it to," the artist suggested.

I groaned and rolled my eyes.

Jason snickered, nudging my elbow again.

"You're an asshole," I muttered. "I hope next time you order steak, it comes with six inches of mushrooms piled on top."

He gasped theatrically. "You take. That. *Back*."

I met him with a challenging look, trying desperately not to laugh. "Or what?"

"Or I'll…" He sputtered a little, then blurted out, "Or next time I go get Subway for the clinic, I'll have them put extra onions on your sandwich."

I narrowed my eyes. "You wouldn't."

He narrowed his right back. "*Triple* onions."

We held each other's glares. Then we both burst out laughing, bumping shoulders as we nearly tumbled off the chairs. Everyone else probably thought we were nuts—weaponizing food topics wasn't *that* funny—but it felt good to laugh like this.

And with Jason…

This felt normal.

This was us. All the time. At work. At lunch. On those rare occasions when I did go out with everyone sans Mark. When we didn't have to be on our best behavior to appease my cranky ex, we laughed. We joked. We teased each other playfully—nothing mean or below the belt. There wasn't a photo in existence of the two of us where I wasn't laughing my head off because he would always say something to make me crack up just before the picture was taken.

Except when Mark was around, of course. But there weren't a lot of pictures of Jason and me during that time—not even group shots or candids—because… Well, because of Mark.

But Mark wasn't here anymore. It was me and Jason and this relaxed, playful fun that I was starting to think I could absolutely lose myself in.

We chuckled and snickered throughout the whole process until the artist announced he was finished.

"Okay." Jason stood and grinned. "Let's see how he drew us."

I returned the grin. "Let's do it."

We went around behind the easel, and as soon as I saw the picture, my heart skipped.

With as ridiculous as we'd been, I genuinely expected us to be portrayed as somber and serious.

On the page, we were...

Exactly like we'd been in the chairs.

Frozen in time, drawn as cartoons, but distinctly *us*, looking at each other and laughing uproariously. Two men having the absolute time of their lives, making each other smile, leaning into each other. If not for the stylized proportions, it could've been a photo.

Jason eyed the artist. "How did you know we were nurses?"

Nurses? What was he—

But then I saw it. I'd been so fixated in our expressions, I hadn't noticed our clothes. We were both dressed in blue scrubs, a stethoscope draped around my neck and an iPad tucked under Jason's arm.

The artist just smiled and shrugged. "A guess."

A guess? Those were some oddly specific things to just guess.

Jason and I exchanged glances but shrugged and took our drawing so the next customer could take our place. Enough weird stuff happened at this carnival, I probably shouldn't have been surprised, but admittedly, I was.

"This blows my mind." I stared at the drawing as we walked away from the booth.

"Right?" Jason looked over my shoulder, and we both stopped. "It's... I mean, it's really good! But the other night..."

I nodded slowly. "The other night, he drew us all opposite who we actually are. Today, he draws us laughing and dressed for work. That's...dude, that's nuts."

Jason's expression turned contemplative. For a long moment, he stared at the caricature, chewing the inside of his cheek.

"Hey." I nudged him gently with my elbow. "What's on your mind?"

"I'm starting to think…" His lips quirked. Then he met my gaze. "I don't think he really draws people the opposite of the way they are."

I cocked my head. "What do you mean?"

"I mean…" Jason seemed to consider it. "Well, okay, drawing Tina as a drunk isn't really a thing. So I don't know what that was all about. But that first night?" He shrugged apologetically. "You really did seem as sad as you looked in the drawing."

I straightened. "Did I?"

"Yeah," he said softly. "Like you could put on a smile and be the life of the party like always, but…I don't know. You just didn't seem happy that night." He paused, then added, "You never really seemed happy when you were out with him."

"Damn. Yeah, he probably saw it. Guess I wasn't very good at hiding it."

"Except you were. Mostly."

"Or not. And what about yours?" I studied him. "You were all…" I gestured around my head. "Hearts and… What was that all about?"

Jason broke eye contact and shrugged again, the gesture tighter than before. "Don't know. I'm still trying to figure that out."

Why don't I believe you?

He cleared his throat. "Want to go check out some of the rides?"

Okay, now I believed him even less, but I didn't push the issue. Whatever it was, he didn't want to talk about it, so I let it go.

"Sure." I swung my backpack around to my elbow and started to unzip it. "Let me just put this away." As I slipped the drawing into the pack, I noticed the other picture I'd forgotten I was carrying around.

So apparently we'd succeeded in shifting our focus away from hunting down the button game to return this damn thing. Still hadn't stumbled across the game yet, though we'd been sitting at the caricaturist's booth for a long time, so we hadn't really had much opportunity.

I let that go, too. I was enjoying myself with Jason.

The cursed painting in my bag would keep.

CHAPTER 13

Jason

My stomach was tight and my balance was off, and I didn't think it had anything to do with that semi-violent spinning ride we'd just stepped out of. Especially since I'd felt about the same way before the ride had started.

In fact, I'd pretty much felt it ever since I'd laid eyes on the newest picture that was now in Ahmed's backpack. Between the two drawings that caricaturist had done of me, I felt stripped bare. Like someone had looked right into me and seen things no one was supposed to know about.

And now that the artist had seen them, I didn't want to keep them hidden anymore. Especially not after the way he'd drawn Ahmed on two separate occasions. Was I reading too much into it? How miserable and depressed his first image had been, compared to how happy he'd looked the second time around? Or how much he'd looked like *himself* in the one tonight? I wanted to dig into it and find out what it all meant, but I was afraid to, and what was I even supposed to say? That a carnival caricaturist saw things we both tried to hide or weren't even aware of? That sounded absolutely insane.

Sort of like cursed paintings that kept reappearing.

And telekinetic goldfish.

And ATMs that I swear to God were *not* right over there a minute ago.

Was I losing my mind? Was I—

"Jason?" Ahmed's gentle voice jarred me out of my thoughts. When had he stopped walking? When had I? How long had we been standing here, off to the side of the flow of traffic, unmoving while people rushed past us?

He touched my shoulder. "Are you okay? You kind of zoned out." With a cautious little smirk, he said, "That ride didn't make you sick, did it?"

I laughed, which got some breath moving. "What? No! The rides here aren't *that* bad." They were intense, but the roller coasters at the nearby amusement park were on another level, and I rode those all the time without issue.

Ahmed's brow pinched. "So if it wasn't the ride, what is it? You okay?"

"I, um…" I chewed my lip. The words wanted to jump right out into the open where I couldn't yank them back. But would that be a mistake? Ahmed had trusted me when he thought he was losing his mind, so maybe he wouldn't judge me over this, but it seemed…more personal. More like I was making assumptions, or—

"Hey." He squeezed my shoulder, forehead creased with concern. Withdrawing his hand, he said, "Talk to me. What's up?"

"I…" Oh, fuck it. Before I could talk myself out of it, I blurted, "I know what our caricatures meant the first night."

Ahmed quirked a brow. "You do?"

"Yeah." I couldn't look at him, so I stared down at the

144

popcorn-littered ground at our feet. "It's… Because the thing is, I can't stop thinking about how he drew Tina. And to be honest, the more I think about it, the more I wonder if we need to see if she's okay."

"Why's that?"

I moistened my lips. "Because the guy drew her as a drunk. Maybe…" I hesitated. "Maybe he saw something we don't. Maybe she has a problem that she's keeping hidden from the rest of us."

"You think so?"

"It would explain why she's had such horrible headaches and felt so awful some days, and why she's so cagey when Lucas tries to figure out what's wrong."

Ahmed's eyes lost focus and his lips parted. "Oh. Wow." He furrowed his brow as he seemed to run through something in his mind. Maybe rewinding some memories and casting them in a different light. Meeting my gaze again, he said, "Do you think so?"

"Yeah, I do," I whispered. Sudden nerves had my heart going wild and my stomach somersaulting, but I barreled on: "Because that artist wasn't drawing people the opposite of the way they really are."

Ahmed shifted his weight. "So he saw me being unhappy with Mark. And Mark being…" He rolled his eyes and waved a hand. "Mark."

"Exactly." I took a deep breath. "He also saw me. The way no one else in the group saw me." I swallowed. "Because I made sure no one saw it."

"He drew you…" Ahmed's eyes went unfocused again for a second, then met mine. "With all the hearts and stuff. That's…" He blinked, and a grin slowly formed. "Wait, did you meet someone and not tell us? Why wouldn't you say anything?"

"I, um…" I dropped my gaze again as heat bloomed in my

cheeks. "I met someone a long time ago. I'm… God, Ahmed. I'm absolutely head over heels in love with someone. But I couldn't say anything. To anyone."

Ahmed sobered. I wasn't looking at him, but I could feel it, and when he spoke, his voice didn't hold a trace of amusement. "Why couldn't you say anything?"

My heart was absolutely slamming into my ribs now, and it took everything I had to look him in the eyes. Somehow, my voice carried over the noise of the carnival going on around us: "Because he was with someone else."

"He was—" Ahmed's teeth snapped together. "Jason, are you…"

"The artist saw it," I whispered. "I've done everything I could for the past three years to hide it from everyone, but he saw right through me."

Ahmed stared at me with wide eyes. "What are you saying?" He knew. He had to. He was too smart and too perceptive not to see where this was going. But maybe he didn't want to assume. Or he was as disbelieving as his startled expression suggested, and he actually needed me to spell it out.

Either way, I'd been holding this card tightly to my vest for a long, long time, and I suddenly *needed* to say it out loud.

"I've been in love with you since forever, Ahmed. I would never in a million years have done anything to interfere with your relationship or make you choose or…" I gestured sharply. "No way. You're my friend first. Always. But I've had a crush on you since the day I met you, and the more I got to know you…" I shook my head and breathed a quiet laugh. "How could I *not* fall for you?"

Ahmed was still silent. Still watching me.

"That artist," I went on, "he saw it. He saw right through me to how much I love you. And it *killed* me that he also saw how miserable you were, because I saw that, too. I've seen it for a long time. I've wished for years I could be the one to make you happy, and not just because Mark obviously didn't want to."

He stayed quiet a second longer, but only a second.

I mean, he was quiet…but he didn't stay still.

With one step, he closed the distance between us, and before I could make sense of anything…

Oh my God.

Those lips were even softer than I'd imagined. The press of his body against mine had me wavering on my feet, and my hands—moving like they had a mind of their own—landed on his waist. Then drifted around to his back.

Holy hell. I'd hugged him countless times over the years, so his shape wasn't unfamiliar, but I'd never held him like *this*. Never while his lips gently teased mine apart. Never while his beard brushed my chin. Sure as shit not seconds after I'd bared my heart to him.

The way his fingers slid up into my hair electrified every nerve ending so strongly I was legitimately surprised every light bulb in the carnival didn't explode. Or maybe they did. I don't think I'd have noticed, because even with all the noise and movement and sounds all around us, even with all those distinctive scents on the air, my entire universe concentrated itself into this. Into us. Into a single point of existence, with everything else blinking out in an instant as if someone had shut off the carnival's power.

Ahmed touched his forehead to mine, and his breath gusted across my lips as he murmured, "I feel so stupid."

That brought me up short. "What?" I drew back and brushed a few strands of dark hair out of his face. "Why?"

His cheeks colored, and he avoided my eyes for a few seconds before, with what seemed like some serious effort, meeting my gaze. "I wasted so much time with him when I could've been with you instead."

"Don't fixate on that." I ran my fingers through his hair, loving the way he shivered and leaned into my touch. "It's the past."

"But I hate that we lost so much time." His fingertips trailed down my cheek. "I had no idea you were into me, and—"

"You weren't supposed to know," I whispered. "You were with someone else. I had to respect that."

Ahmed frowned. "I get it. I'm not upset at you. I'm upset at myself for not figuring out that—I mean, not that you had feelings for me, but just that it should've been a huge goddamned red flag that I enjoyed spending time with you more than with my boyfriend. I should've known I was miserable with him, and I lost so damn much time with you, and—"

I kissed him gently, and as it lingered, he slowly relaxed against me. "We can't change the past," I whispered. "But if you want to make up for lost time, say the word."

He held my gaze. His eyes were always so damn beautiful, but right now, they were gleaming with more heat and desire than I'd ever fantasized about him directing at me. Then he licked his lips. "Would it be weird if I said I wanted to get the hell out of here?"

Oh. Fuck.

I gulped. "I'm assuming you're not suddenly in the mood for a slice of pie at the café."

Ahmed's easy laughter lit up the whole night all over again. "No. Definitely not." His eyes flicked to my lips, and when they came back up to meet my gaze again, they smoldered with something unmistakable. "My place? Because I don't think your roommates would be too happy with us."

I blinked. He was really suggesting… He wanted…

He lifted his chin and kissed me again, and his voice was husky with want as he murmured, "Let's get out of here."

Oh, hell yeah.

But I didn't move. "What about the painting? The sooner we get rid of it—"

"I don't care." He shook his head as he laced our fingers together. "If it pulls some more cursed nonsense on the way home, then we'll just screw in the bed of your truck while we wait for roadside."

I blinked. "Seriously?"

"Seriously."

"Well, hell." I squeezed his hand and started heading toward the exit. "What are we waiting for?"

His laughter was the most amazing sound I'd ever heard.

CHAPTER 14

Ahmed

I was fully prepared for the ride home to take for-fucking-ever.

The field where the carnival was held wasn't exactly around the corner from my apartment. That ribbon of highway between there and town? It stretched out for a *while*. And there was also that part where I was beyond desperate to get Jason behind closed doors and out of his clothes.

So as he pulled out of the parking lot with me in the passenger seat of his truck and his kiss still tingling on my lips, I was already starting to lose my mind. There was no way I could wait as long as it would take to get us back to my place.

Maybe we could just stop along the way. Make good on my suggestion to jump into the bed of his truck and hope nobody happened by while we were going at it. Because I wanted him. Holy hell, I wanted him. This drive—it was going to drive me insane, that was what it was going to do.

Except…

We were here. At my apartment.

What the fuck?

I glanced to my left as Jason pulled into the vacant parking spot beside my car.

Did...did that just happen?

This wasn't like when I drove on autopilot, then snapped out of it and realized I'd zoned out and didn't remember driving from point A to point B. It was like I blinked and was just...here.

But I didn't spend too much time thinking about it because we were getting out of Jason's truck, and if the universe had seen fit to teleport us home or some shit, cool. Of all the absolutely bizarre things that had happened in recent days, this one was among the best, so I wasn't going to look this weird gift horse in the mouth.

Our eyes met as we came around the front of his truck. We exchanged grins, then headed inside.

When we stopped outside my door, Jason said, "Funny— the drive didn't take as long as I thought it would." He chuckled. "Good thing there were no cops, or I'd have a nasty ticket."

I just laughed as I fumbled with my keys. "Guess we got lucky."

"Nah." He slid his hands over my waist and kissed the side of my neck. In a low, sultry voice, he purred, "We're gonna get lucky once you get that door open."

I snorted. A hot breath of laughter rushed across my neck, giving me goose bumps and making me forget how to work a key or a lock or a stupid doorknob.

"Need a hand?" he teased.

Probably, yeah, but like hell was I going to let on that I couldn't operate a door. "I've got it."

"You sure?" His slid his hands into my front pockets and

pressed against my ass, letting me feel the erection that was as steel-hard as my own.

"Goddammit, Jason…" I fumbled with my keys again. He laughed against my neck again. Dizzy, chuckling, and maybe a little frustrated, I muttered, "You suck."

Another huff of laughter. "Okay, now you're just setting me up for the jokes."

I closed my eyes and let my forehead touch the door. "Oh my God."

He snickered. Then he gently turned me around by the hips, pressed me up against the door, and kissed me with a kind of hunger that no one had ever directed at me before. As if he needed my kiss like he needed air, his hands trembling against the sides of my neck as he gently but eagerly explored my mouth.

When he broke that kiss with a gasp, he touched his forehead to mine and panted hard against my lips, all teasing gone from his voice. "I'm sorry. I'm… I just couldn't wait. I wanted—"

I claimed his mouth again, reveling in his soft whimper and the way his whole body seemed to respond, somehow tensing and relaxing all at once. "Don't apologize," I whispered. "Just let me get the door open."

He nodded, loosening his hold on me. "Okay." Eyes flicking from side to side, he sheepishly added, "Probably shouldn't let your neighbors catch us."

I laughed as I turned to unlock the door. "It'll be payback for the six months it took for some of them to figure out how thin the walls are."

"Oh yeah? Do I want to know?"

I shrugged, biting back a *"thank fuck"* when I managed to actually work the deadbolt. As I opened the door, I said, "Let's just say his wife's a screamer and they like to watch their porn on max volume."

Jason barked a laugh as he followed me into the apartment. As he shut and locked the door behind him, he asked, "Sooo...does that mean we should put on a porno for ambiance while we try to make each other scream?"

I tossed my keys on the counter, then pressed him up against the door just like he'd done to me. "I don't need any ambiance, and I'm planning to keep your mouth too busy for you to scream."

I had about two nanoseconds to cringe at how utterly cheesy that sounded. Maybe three.

But then Jason shivered, curving a hand behind my neck and drawing me in, and a low growl came from his throat as he kissed me, hard and greedy. Maybe the comment had been cheesy, but it obviously didn't bother him, and I was too caught up in his gently assertive mouth to worry about anything else.

Jason sucked in a sharp breath through his nose and gripped me tighter as he squirmed between my body and the door, and I realized I'd unconsciously started rubbing against him, desperate for some friction on my dick. It was too late to even bother wanting to apologize or thinking he wouldn't like it—not when he very clearly did and was egging me on.

Everything I did to telegraph what I wanted—it didn't annoy him or frustrate him. No, it turned him on and sent him even higher. Made him hold me closer. Kiss me harder. Grind right back against me as if he needed and wanted this just as much as I did.

Fuck—Jason really wanted me. He'd said as much, and so had the way he'd kissed me at the carnival, but right now... Oh my God. I'd been with guys who wanted me, but Jason was an absolute wreck for me. A shaking, moaning, utterly hopeless wreck who touched me and tasted me like he couldn't begin to get enough, and nothing in the world had ever been headier.

After so much time wasted thinking I was, at best, worthy of a few scraps of affection, here was my best friend in the world, trembling with need. For *me*.

What if he wakes up tomorrow, decides that was all he needed, and moves on?

The thought tried to intrude and dump cold water over my arousal, but I ignored it. Maybe he would. Maybe this was all he wanted, and we'd be back to friends and coworkers tomorrow. Wouldn't be the first time someone was more into the thrill of the hunt than actually being with me.

If that was the case, I'd notch that bedpost when I got to it.

For tonight...

Fuck, I was going to drown in everything Jason was willing to offer, and I was going to try my damnedest to give him the pleasure and satisfaction he deserved.

Even if all I can have is tonight, let's make it amazing.

I broke the kiss and met his gaze. Jesus, this was a side of Jason I'd never even let myself imagine. All want and hunger, eyes gleaming with bliss and desire, lips kiss-swollen and parted as he tried to catch his breath.

"We should..." I paused to catch my own breath. "Bedroom?"

He licked his lips and nodded. "Love that idea."

"Figured you'd be on board." I slid my hand into his and led him down toward the hallway.

In the living room, he paused, glancing at the stack of boxes. "Is that Mark's crap?"

I shook my head. "Nah, it's some stuff he grabbed by accident and brought back. I just haven't had a chance to unpack it yet."

"Aw. Damn."

"What?" I eyed him. "You're disappointed my ex's stuff is gone?"

"No." He nudged me back against the wall and dipped his head to kiss my neck. "I just thought if it *was* his stuff, you could fuck me over the stack before he comes to pick it up."

Delirious laughter bubbled up as I tilted my head to let him explore my neck. "You're such a dork."

"Uh-huh. But it would be funny, wouldn't it?"

"Okay, I'll give you that." Hot, too. Mostly because it would mean I was fucking Jason, and at this point, the venue for that seriously didn't matter. I carded my fingers through his hair. "I don't want to think about him right now."

"Pretty sure I can keep your mind off him." Jason lifted his head and kissed me, and...keep my mind off who?

It wasn't just his kiss. Now that there was no one around to catch us, he didn't hold back anymore. His hands were all over me—my hair, my back, my ass—sliding over my clothes like he just needed to feel me and make sure this was real. I could relate. I dragged my fingers and palms all over every inch of him I could reach, committing him to memory as if I might suddenly wake up from this dream and never touch him again.

"Bed...bedroom," I stammered. "We should... God, Jason..."

His breath stuttered across my skin when I said his name. Lifting his head, he met my gaze, and the heat in his eyes almost had me melting to the floor. No one had ever looked at me like that—hungry and longing and on fucking fire with need— and it was off-the-charts sexy.

Definitely needed to be in the bedroom. Like *now*.

We made it there, finally, and somehow—God only knew how—we managed to strip our clothes off in between kissing and groping. Before the last piece of clothing had even landed on the floor, I pulled Jason down onto my bed, my pulse soaring as his narrow hips settled between my thighs. His kiss, his warmth, his naked skin against mine—this was hardly my first time in bed with a man, but it was the first time with Jason, and that was dizzying and overwhelming.

I'd been eager and frantic to get in here and get him naked, but now that he was, everything…slowed down. The urgency hadn't been to get off and be done with it—it had been for this. For exactly what we were doing now: touching and kissing with nothing but heat between us. Yes, I needed friction, and Jason rocked his hips just right to satisfy that need, but what I wanted more than anything was to just hold on and explore him and feel him. I wanted to be needed like this for the first time in my life, and Jason delivered in spades, his kisses worshipful and his touches tender and maybe a little disbelieving, as if this felt like a dream for him too.

"Jason," I whispered, partly to get his attention and partly just to hear myself saying his name like this.

He pushed himself up and gazed down at me, eyebrows up.

I couldn't resist trailing my fingertips down his cheek. "Are you in any hurry? Because I kind of…kind of like taking it slow."

He grinned. "I do too. And…" He bit his lip, then added a little sheepishly, "I've been wanting this for a long time. Never actually thought it would happen. So I'd like to"—he leaned down to brush a featherlight kiss across my mouth— "savor it."

Then we were kissing again, and his words had me covered in goose bumps. Had I just been with Mark too long? Or had I really never known what it was like for a man to want me so bad he wanted to *savor* it? Whatever—it was heady as hell. Sex was great, but being *craved* like this? Oh hell, I wanted to savor *that*.

Especially since, I'd somehow only discovered today, it turned out I wanted him so bad I ached for him. And now I had him—his touch, his kiss, his desire. Everything was unhurried and perfect. We were both steel-hard, our cocks trapped between our bodies and our hips moving just enough to maintain a dizzying friction, and he held me... reverently? Was that the word? Because no man had ever held me quite like he did now. Close to him, wrapping me up in his strong arms, touching me all over as if he couldn't believe this was real and he wanted to memorize every plane and contour of my body. Maybe *reverently* was the word, because in Jason's arms, I felt absolutely worshipped.

And I hoped my touch and my embrace had the same effect on him. Maybe I'd been slow on the uptake about my feelings and attraction for him, but my eyes were metaphorically wide open now.

Of course I want you.

I've loved you so long I don't remember when I didn't.

The thought almost choked me up. I did love him. I'd known all this time that I loved my friend—that our friendship was special and ran deeper than others I had—but tonight...

I don't know how to say it yet, and maybe it's too soon anyway.

I held him tighter, kissing him hungrily.

But I am absolutely in love with you, Jason.

Neither of us was kidding about taking our time. We spent forever touching and looking at each other in a whole new light. I'd known for a long time that he had a fit physique—not a six-pack or anything, but he was trim and obviously spent time at the gym. We'd been to barbecues and pool parties, so it wasn't like seeing each other shirtless was anything new. It was so different to actually run my hands over those muscles, though.

His tattoo sleeve was always partly visible when he wore

scrubs, and he'd shown me and our coworkers the whole thing before. Plus…barbecues and pool parties. It was hardly anything novel or unfamiliar, but I was fascinated with it anyway. The contrast between the intricate ink and the rest of his fair skin. How some of the lines and edges looked like they should've been raised ridges or grooves but were completely smooth beneath my fingertips. I knew he was the same man I saw in scrubs every single day, but the familiar tattoos made this real. I was in bed with Jason. My coworker. My friend.

You've been right here in front of me all this time.

I slid my hands up his chest, trailing my thumb over the abstract knotwork tattooed on his pec.

How am I only seeing you like this now?

"God, you're gorgeous." The words tumbled out without thought.

He opened his eyes, and though his skin was already flushed with arousal, a blush intensified the color in his cheeks. He smiled, shifting onto one arm so he could touch my face with the other hand. "I've been biting my tongue for three years, but…so are you." He carded his fingers through my hair. "You're fucking beautiful, Ahmed." The words made my eyes sting, but it was the reverence that almost broke me.

"I wish you'd said something sooner," I murmured, again without really thinking about it.

Jason shook his head. "No. I wasn't going to… Not while you were with someone else."

I understood that, and I regretted the comment. "I know. I…I shouldn't have said that. It was—"

"Hey. Hey." He caressed my cheek. "It took us a while to get here because the timing wasn't right before. Now it is." His soft smile was so sexy and sweet, and his voice was full of sincerity as he said, "Everything about you and this was worth the wait."

I squeezed my eyes shut as a sudden flood of emotions threatened to kill the mood. I didn't know which hit me harder—that someone existed who believed I was worth a damn, or that he'd been right in front of my oblivious face all this time.

"Ahmed." He kissed my forehead. "We don't have to do this now if—"

"No." I looked up at him. "I want this. It's just…" I swallowed, not sure how to explain it. But then I remembered who I was with, and who I *wasn't* with, and I realized that telling the God's honest truth wouldn't leave me cold and alone in this bed. Struggling to keep my voice even, I admitted, "It's just overwhelming. Being with someone who wants me like you do."

Multiple emotions flickered through Jason's eyes—one of them anger, I was pretty sure—before he softly asked, "Overwhelming in a good way?"

That almost drove a laugh out of me. Not because it was particularly funny, but because I wasn't sure I knew the words to tell him just how good it was, and because, well…I was overwhelmed.

"It's good." I ran a shaky hand through his hair. "It's really good. Just…a lot. And doing this tonight—yeah, I want it." I drew him back down to me. "I've never wanted anyone like this."

The answer was a ragged breath slipping through the space between our lips, and then he kissed me again. Despite the momentary hiccup, the mood was anything but killed. If anything, the desire burned even hotter now, the kisses deeper and the touches hungrier.

Yes, I still hated that I'd wasted so much time when the perfect man was right here all along, but it couldn't be helped. I was just grateful that he hadn't run out of patience for me, and not a moment too soon, we were here now.

I wanted to get absolutely lost in him.

And I wanted him to be absolutely lost in every bit of pleasure I could give him.

I slid a hand down between us, and Jason hissed a breath as he lifted his hips to give me room. When I closed my fingers around his dick, his eyelids fluttered shut and he moaned something that might've been my name. I wondered if he even knew he was rocking his hips, complementing my slow strokes.

Experimentally, I tightened my grip. Jason's head fell beside mine, a low groan escaping his throat as he started thrusting into my fist.

"Fuck, Ahmed," he breathed. "Oh my God…"

"Tell me what you want," I whispered in his ear. Then, with a grin, I added, "And don't get sappy and say you want me. You know what I mean."

A breathless, almost drunken laugh warmed my shoulder before he pushed himself up and gazed down at me again. "Maybe we should've—" He bit his lip as I ran my thumb over the head of his dick. "Oh Jesus…"

"Maybe we should've, what?" I teased.

He licked his lips and tried again. "Talked in the truck. About…about the things we like. Don't like. That stuff."

He made a valid point, but so did I: "Do you think either of us had enough brain cells to form words on that drive?"

His eyebrow flicked up. "Do you think we do now?" With a pointed downward glance, he added, "Do you think I do while your hand is doing… Oh, fuck. *That?*"

I chuckled. "Not at all. But it's entertaining to watch you try."

Jason laughed, which would've been so out of place with any other man but was so perfect with us. We were relaxed with each other. This was…

It was *easy*.

I took pity on him and stopped stroking his dick. "Tell me," I whispered. "What do you want me to do?"

Jason sobered, "I, um...I usually don't bottom with someone until I've been with them a few times, but..." He grinned. "I could definitely make an exception this time."

Oh, fuck. Just thinking of being balls-deep in Jason had my head spinning. "That could be hot."

"Yeah? Do you top?"

I nodded, and I didn't mention why I hadn't topped in a long time. We didn't need to discuss that other guy right now. Except he was relevant to this moment in other respects. Namely, why I didn't have everything on hand that I'd actually need to top Jason.

"I, um...I don't have any condoms." I licked my lips. Panic rose in my chest along with a certainty he was about to roll his eyes and bail, and I quickly added, "But there's plenty we can do without, so..."

His grin made my toes curl. So did his long, perfect kiss, and then he whispered, "I don't care what we do. I'm with you—this is perfect."

My whole body broke out in goose bumps. "Jason..."

"I know it sounds cheesy." He kissed along my jaw, working his way down to my neck again. "But I mean it. All I want to do is drive you wild. The rest..." He half-shrugged as he met my gaze again. "I want to do everything with you— every goddamned thing in the world—but we don't have to do it all tonight, you know?" There was a hint of hopefulness in his eyes that took my lust-addled brain a second to parse.

We don't have to do it all tonight...because this won't be the last time.

Right?

At this rate, he was going to make me cry before he made me come, and not in a bad way.

Wrapping my arms around him, I drew him back down to

me, and just before our lips met, I whispered, "We have all the time in the world."

The shiver that ran through him spoke of profound relief. As if this all felt precarious to him, and he craved reassurance as much as he craved my touch.

"Jason," I whispered.

He pushed himself up and locked eyes with me. "Hmm?"

I caressed his cheek. "I'm not going anywhere."

His eyebrows flicked up, but then he blushed as he broke eye contact with a self-deprecating laugh. "I'm not usually this..." He swallowed hard.

Concern tightened my chest. "Hmm?"

"It's just... I've wanted you for a long time. But I never thought it was going to happen, you know?" The raw vulnerability in his eyes was as heartbreaking as it was sweet. "Then we suddenly land here, and I'm... I guess I'm afraid I'll blink and it'll be gone."

"It won't." I lifted my head and claimed a long, gentle kiss. Easing back onto the pillow, I whispered, "You're worried we're on thin ice, and I'm over here wondering how the fuck I went his long without realizing how I felt about you."

Disbelief widened his eyes.

"Obviously I was with someone else," I went on. "I wasn't looking for anything because—like, Mark was a jerk, but cheating? That's not me. So I didn't let myself..." I sighed, shaking my head. "But then tonight? As soon as we made that connection, it's like...no shit, I want you. How did I ever think I didn't?"

"Really?"

"Yeah. I mean, on one hand, it feels like this fell out of the sky. But on the other..." I smiled up at him. "I swear, I feel like the whole universe is telling me, 'Jesus Christ, it's about time you caught on, dumbass.'"

Jason's shy but heartfelt laugh made the whole room brighter. "I mean, I wasn't going to say it *quite* like that but—"

"Shut up," I said, chuckling.

He grinned, then came down to kiss me, and even as our amusement faded, the tenderness didn't. He held me—really *held* me—like no one ever had before. He was afraid he'd blink and this would be over? I could relate.

But I wasn't going anywhere, and more and more, I settled into believing that he wasn't either.

"We've got time," I murmured against his lips as I slid my hand up his back. "This isn't a one-night stand."

"No, it isn't," he breathed, and then we were kissing, deep and greedy, our bodies tangling up all over again.

I'd had plenty of first times with guys, but none of them had ever been like this. I was usually quick to sleep with someone new because I didn't want to waste my time dating someone who turned out to be selfish in bed. Been there, regretted that. I was absolutely a sex-on-the-first-date kind of guy, so most of my first times had been with men I only knew from chatting online, a few FaceTime calls, and maybe a date.

Jason... Oh God, my first time with Jason was the first time I'd ever had sex like this.

I knew him. I trusted him. There were no secrets between us. Now that we were in bed, we explored each other with a kind of confidence and easy communication I'd never had with a new partner. If one of us didn't like something, it wasn't going to kill the mood or send the other running for the hills.

There was no hurry, either—not to get ourselves or each other off. This had to be the most relaxed first-time exploration I'd ever experienced, and it was *heaven*. We kissed forever while we stroked each other's dicks between us. I climbed on top and lazily frotted against him while we made out in between gasping and swearing. For ages, we lay on our sides, sixty-nining like we had all the time in the world to taste and tease each other.

Now I was on my back again with Jason's narrow hips between my thighs, and I decided then and there that I would never get tired of the way this man kissed. He was so gentle and perfect—oh my God, I loved this.

Where has sex like this been all my life?

Oh. Right. Two desks over from my office in tattoos and scrubs.

I curved my hands down over his ass, and he growled against my lips. Rocking his hips just right, he rubbed his dick alongside mine, and the room spun around me.

He barely broke the kiss enough to murmur, "Like that?"

"Uh-huh." I squeezed his perfect ass cheeks. "Maybe some lube, though?"

"Ooh, good idea." He sat up, glanced around, then zeroed in on the nightstand. "Ah. There it is." He grabbed it, and we turned on our sides so neither of us had to worry about staying balanced.

In no time, we both had some lube on our hands. I had my hand on his dick first, and with one stroke, I had Jason trembling, a breathy "Oh, God," rolling off his lips. Then his fingers were around my cock, and I was the one shaking and slurring. I didn't think I'd ever been this keyed up from a handjob. It usually took me forever to come this way unless I was doing it myself.

Tonight, that was not going to be a problem.

"Oh my God," Jason whispered. "Still can't believe…" He trailed off, but I knew what he meant. He gave his strokes a little twist, driving me higher, and somehow he managed to keep talking. "I've wanted you since forever," he panted, thrusting hard against me. "Not gonna lie—I've…fantasized…" He bit his lip as his eyelids slid closed. "Fuck…"

An image flickered through my mind of Jason jerking

himself off to thoughts of us together, and my breath hitched. "Have you?"

"So much," he murmured. "And the real deal is…" Another shudder, harder this time, and he tilted his head back with a soft groan. Then he pushed me onto my back again, and as we pumped each other between our bodies, every muscle in his neck and shoulders stood out, and his voice was a ragged whisper: "This is a million times better than my fantasies."

I moaned, arching beneath him. I hadn't thought to fantasize about him, but I could say without a doubt that any fantasy I'd ever had would never have come close to this reality. Nothing I'd ever conjured in my mind—not even my hottest mental pornos that had driven me to earth-shaking orgasms—had ever been as spine-meltingly hot as sex with Jason.

And neither of us had even come yet.

"Baby…" I dragged my free hand through his sweat-dampened hair. "I wanna…I wanna make you come."

Teeth grazed my shoulder. "You're gonna. Holy shit, Ahmed…"

No one had ever made my name sound so simultaneously sexy and profane. I loved it.

"Let me get on top," I whispered.

He kissed the spot he'd bitten. Then he came up and kissed my mouth, and when our eyes met… Jesus. I wondered if it would ever stop being a novelty to see so much desire smoldering in those beautiful eyes. I hoped not —I wanted it to straight up take my breath away every damn time.

He dusted another kiss across my lips, and then we changed positions. He lay back, I straddled him, and after I'd put some more lube on my hand, I closed my fingers around both our dicks.

"Oh God," he groaned, arching under us. "Fuck…"

I couldn't get enough of watching him come unraveled, so I let go of my cock and focused on his, pumping him hard and fast as he arched and writhed under me. Christ, he was mesmerizing, and watching him unravel from my ministrations made me dizzy with lust. It didn't matter why it had taken me so damn long to realize how hot he was—I realized it now, and I suddenly wanted his orgasm more than I'd ever wanted my own.

Show me how beautiful you are when you come.

He didn't keep me waiting long. His breathing became rapid and shallow, and he squeezed his eyes shut as he thrust into my fist, his lips moving in soundless cries as a flush crept down his neck and chest.

"Don't stop," he pleaded, pushing himself up on his elbow as if he just needed to *move.* "Oh my God…" His hand landed on my shoulder, and his fingertips twitched as his cock stiffened in my grip and his head fell back. "I'm so… Right there. Oh, yeah, I'm—"

Then his whole body jerked, and he gave the most delicious, throaty cry as he dropped back onto the mattress and cum shot onto his stomach.

It said more about men I'd been with before than about the man I was with now, but I had a flash of disappointment, thinking that since he got off first, I was probably on my own. That had happened more times than I cared to think about.

Somehow it was both a pleasant surprise and the most natural, predictable thing in the world when Jason whispered, "Let me clean this off, and then you're all mine."

The word *"Really?"* almost popped out of my mouth, but I managed to keep it back. Of course, really. All my past bullshit aside, Jason had made it undeniably clear that he was in this for me as much as himself.

And when he came back from the bathroom, he made

good on that promise. After spending ages exploring my mouth like it was the first time all over again, he started kissing down my neck and my chest, and I had a feeling I knew where he was headed.

"The lube," I murmured. "It doesn't taste…uh…" Words? What were words?

"Don't care what it tastes like." He ran the tip of his tongue around my nipple. "You have no idea how high *suck Ahmed off* has been on my list of things I wish I could do." He glanced up at me, a wicked grin on his lips. "It's going to take a lot more than a little bit of lube to scare me away from doing that that."

He wasn't kidding—if the taste of the lube bothered him, he definitely didn't let on. He'd been languid and explorative when he'd teased me earlier and when we'd sixty-nined, but now he was a man on a mission, and I had no idea how I didn't levitate off the bed from pure bliss. His tongue was absolutely magic. His lips had driven me wild while we kissed, and they were spectacular on my dick. The low groans, the way his fingertips teased my balls, the little glances every now and then as if he wanted to see exactly what he was doing to me—it was like he effortlessly intuited everything that would send me into the stratosphere.

"That's it," I breathed. "God, Jason. Make me come. *Please.*"

He moaned as he deep-throated me, and then he was pumping me hard as his lips and tongue focused on the head of my cock, and he had me so close, but suddenly I needed more.

"Get up here and kiss me," I demanded. "Get—fuck. Jason, I need your mouth."

He didn't argue. A second later, he was over me, his hand pumping my spit-slicked dick as he kissed me greedily and messily. He'd driven me wild blowing me, but his kiss had me halfway out of my mind, and with the way he was going to town on my mouth and jerking me off for all he was worth, my orgasm was closing in fast.

I wanted to come. Needed to come. Fucking ached to come.

But Jason didn't let me. Not quite yet. He got me right to the edge…right there…just shy of the point of no return…and he kept me there. Held me there. Let me teeter precariously there while I gasped and tried to find enough breath to beg for release, and his lips landed on my throat and—

"Fuck!" My entire body was pure electricity for a few perfect heartbeats, and Jason kept stroking and teasing until I started to come back down.

"Jesus, you're so beautiful," he whispered. "If I hadn't come already, this would've had me there in a heartbeat."

I shivered, still shaking from my orgasm and now from his words. "Holy shit."

He laughed softly and kissed my cheek. "So damn gorgeous."

"And so damn covered in cum."

We both snorted. He kissed me gently, still grinning. "I'm not going to bitch about seeing you covered in cum." He nipped my lower lip. "Though I wouldn't mind seeing you covered in *my* cum."

I blinked. "Nurse Richards, you have a filthy mouth!"

"Uh-huh. And?"

"Just saying. By all means, carry on."

"That's what I thought."

We laughed in between kissing lazily. Eventually I did get up to clean myself off, and when I settled back into bed, I was right where I hadn't realized until tonight I ached to be—wrapped up in Jason's strong arms. He held me, stroking my hair, and we were back to lazy, gentle kissing. Maybe we'd go another round tonight. Maybe we wouldn't. Honestly, I didn't care, because this wasn't a one-night stand. This wouldn't be the last time.

This was perfect, and somehow, it was real.

Lying here like this, warm and blissed out with the sweetest man I'd ever met, I could barely imagine a world where this *wasn't* my reality. How had it only been tonight that we'd kissed for the first time? This felt as brand new as it was, but also seemed like it had been inevitable. Or like we'd been this way all along.

Or maybe my orgasm had fried some circuitry in my head, and now I couldn't think clearly anymore. No complaints here.

Closing my eyes, I sighed happily as I held him closer.

I had no idea everything I wanted in a man was right in front of my face.

But now that you're here...

I can't imagine wanting anyone else.

CHAPTER 15

Jason

This wasn't real. There was no way it had actually happened. I was clearly in the throes of the flu and having a vivid fever dream. One in which I was lying with Ahmed after we'd rumpled his sheets and made each other come.

Except…no. Everything about this was crystal clear in a way no dream ever was. I was aware of everything: his warm skin touching mine. His cool hair between my lazily stroking fingers. The pleasant drowsiness that always followed an orgasm. Distant sounds of life going on outside—activity in neighboring apartments, voices in the parking lot, cars going by.

No fever. No dream.

We were really here.

Beside me, Ahmed yawned. Then he stretched and turned onto his side, pushing himself up on his elbow. With the most adorably sleepy expression, he said, "Damn. I almost fell asleep."

"You can go to sleep." I ran my knuckles down the middle of his chest just because I could. "I probably won't be too far behind."

A shy smile slowly materialized. "So if I said I wanted you to stay the rest of the night instead of taking off..."

The feeling that rose in my chest was right up there with being a kid who'd just realized Santa brought him everything he'd asked for. By some miracle, though, I held on to my dignity. "I don't have anywhere else to be."

The laugh was soft and genuine, but I swore it might have been hiding some relief. As if he actually thought I was in a hurry to be anywhere but here. "Good. Because you never know—I might have enough in me for another round."

"Ooh, well, now I should definitely stay." I pushed myself up a little and kissed him lightly. "Seriously, though, I don't have anywhere else to be." It took all the restraint I had not to tell him I'd been waiting ages to get here—I'd stay as long as he wanted me to.

Ahmed smiled, and he let another kiss linger for a moment before we both settled onto the pillows again, facing each other on our sides. He laced our fingers together between our chests, and when his eyes met mine again, he'd turned serious. "So...where do we go from here?"

Oh. That.

I swallowed. "Don't know. What do you think?" Probably a coward's move, punting the ball back to him, but I was *terrified* of saying the wrong thing and spooking him away from me. I still couldn't quite believe we'd made it to this, and it felt weirdly precarious, even though I knew, rationally, that Ahmed wasn't one to bolt at the slightest provocation. We'd had disagreements throughout our friendship—even a few mildly heated ones—and he'd always been the cooler head who was willing to talk things through. Even if we didn't quite see eye to eye on something in the end, it had never threatened our friendship.

Why should that be any different now that we'd taken things to this level?

No idea, but I really, really didn't want to screw this up, so before I put my foot in my mouth, I waited to see where *he* thought we should go from here.

He seemed to consider it for a moment, watching his thumb run back and forth along mine. After a while, he met my gaze. "I don't know? I've never done this before. With someone I was already close to. So I have no idea what qualifies as too fast or too slow or…" He rolled his eyes and gave a self-deprecating laugh. "No idea."

I laughed too, but it was relief on my part. "That makes two of us, I guess."

"Yeah?"

I nodded. "The closest I've ever come to it was when Peyton and I dated, but nothing really came of that."

An odd smile quirked his lips. "You know, I always wondered what happened between you two."

Cheeks warming, I half-shrugged. "Nothing really dramatic. We gave it a try—a few tries, actually—but it became pretty clear we were better off staying friends."

"Why's that?"

"Just…" I chewed the inside of my cheek. "I don't really know how to describe it. There was some chemistry, and we really like each other, but whenever we tried to date, we'd end up butting heads. So after a few tries, we decided to be friends."

"Ah, okay. Yeah, I could see that killing things. I'm glad you stayed friends, though."

"Oh, yeah, we were fine. We were both on the same page about it, and there weren't any hard feelings. In fact, we were having dinner when we talked about it, and we still ended up going to the concert and having some drinks later. Just, you know, as friends. Once we decided, okay, this isn't going to work romantically, the pressure was off and we were good."

Ahmed smiled. "Good. With as close as you are to them it would've been a shame to lose that."

"Exactly." I looked in those dark eyes that had scrambled my brain so damn many times. "I didn't want to screw up my friendship with them, and I don't want to screw ours up either." I brought our hands up and pressed a soft kiss to his knuckles. "How do we do that?"

"I don't know," he whispered. "I didn't realize until tonight that I wanted this at all, and now it just seems so damn obvious. You're my best friend, and we're..." He blushed. "We've definitely got some chemistry."

Goose bumps sprang up along my back. "Yeah, we do. We can take this a day at a time, though. It doesn't need a name or anything right this second." I swept my tongue across my lips. "And you also just broke up with someone. If you want to take some time to move on after him, I'll—"

"Fuck no." He squeezed my hand, then lifted his chin and kissed me lightly. "I wasted enough time on him. Honestly? I think I mentally checked out of that relationship a long time ago."

"Really?"

Ahmed nodded. "I didn't realize it because...I don't know. Denial, I guess? And even when I considered breaking things off with him a few times, I couldn't drop the hammer because confrontation with him is...ugh. It's such a fucking headache."

"It was easier to stay with him than break up with him?"

He seemed to think about it, then shrugged. "Kind of, yeah? I know it sounds stupid, but arguing with him..." Ahmed rolled his eyes and groaned. "Oh my God, it sucked. And like, yeah, it hurt when he left. It was a relief, but it also hurt. It... I guess that doesn't make much sense, but there it is."

"It doesn't have to make sense." I ran my fingertips along his arm. "You feel what you feel."

Nodding, he said, "Yeah. Emotions are weird. After the dust settled a bit, though, it was a bigger relief than anything. Especially since there's no telling how long it would've taken my coward ass to work up the courage to dump him, and I feel like he's the kind of guy who doesn't just ride off into the sunset unless he's the one to initiate the breakup."

"*Ugh*, people like that *suck*." I rolled my eyes. "Been there."

He studied me, then grimaced. "Oh, right. How long did it take Daniel to leave you alone?"

"Too long," I grumbled. "Maybe I should've just pissed him off until he dumped me, and then he'd have flounced out of the picture for good." I paused. "That sounds underhanded and manipulative, doesn't it?"

"It does, but I get it. I think that's basically what I did with Mark, even if I wasn't thinking about it consciously. I didn't know how to leave so we could have a clean break, so I just... stopped being the person he wanted to be with until he finally left." Ahmed wrinkled his nose. "It does sound kind of fucked up when you say it out loud, doesn't it?"

I chuckled. "Kind of. But it makes sense. Sometimes you have to do whatever it takes to get out of a bad situation."

"Yeah. Still, I just... Ugh. I wish I'd had the spine to dump his ass ages ago. Then maybe we could've..." He trailed off, shaking his head.

"Just meant we had more time to be friends."

Ahmed studied me.

I smiled. "We've spent the last three years working together and becoming good friends. There was none of that best-behavior bullshit everyone does at the beginning of a relationship. We spend like fifty hours a week together, and we've seen each other in every mood imaginable. We've butted heads and argued, so we know we can disagree and come back from it." I shrugged as I stroked his cheek. "We're not diving into a new relationship with someone we just met. We're... I guess we're upgrading a friendship that's already on rock-solid ground."

For a moment, I wasn't sure what he'd think of that. If it was too much, or the wrong thing, or—

Ahmed smiled.

His smile had always liquefied me, but this time it was on the heels of me telling him all that, and it was heady and a relief and so damn adorable.

"I like that," he whispered, caressing my cheek. "Upgrading our friendship?"

My heart went wild. We were really doing this? Holy shit! "I like it, too."

The smile brightened, but faltered. "Just be patient with me." He ran his fingers through my hair. "I'm glad to be out of the relationship with Mark, but there's still..."

"There's still a lot to work through," I said softly. "I get it. And there's no pressure from me."

He watched me uncertainly.

"I mean it." I lifted my chin and pressed a gentle kiss to his lips. "I wouldn't put any pressure on you as a friend. That doesn't change when I'm your—" I hesitated, not sure what to call us yet.

"Boyfriend?" he offered with what I thought was hope.

"Works for me," I said cautiously. "Whatever the label, it still stands—no pressure. Not for us, and not for moving on after him."

"Thank you." He stole a soft kiss. "What about at work?"

"At—oh. Yeah. I guess we should figure that out." I drew him closer and slid my hand down his back. "I don't care if anyone knows. It isn't like it's against the rules."

"True. And our friends will figure it out soon enough."

I groaned and rolled my eyes. "Oh God. Lucas is going to be insufferable. And when he tells Peyton…" I grimaced.

Ahmed's eyebrow flicked up. "You think Peyton will have an issue with it?"

"No, no. Not at all." I chuckled. "They've just had to listen to me pining for you for the last couple of years, and they were absolutely sure that if Mark was ever out of the picture…"

Ahmed eyed me just long enough to think it might not have been a good idea to tell him that, but then he laughed. "Knowing them, I think you're going to be hearing 'I told you so' for a long time."

"Right?" I tsked, but smiled. "I can live with it, though."

"Oh yeah?"

"Well, yeah." I grinned even as heat rose in my cheeks. "There are worse things to be wrong about than 'Ahmed isn't interested in me like that.'"

"Hmm, good point." He pushed himself up and rolled me onto my back, and as he climbed on top, he said, "For the record, then…" He came down to kiss me as we both started to firm up between our bodies. "I can say with absolute authority…" He brushed his lips across mine "…that Ahmed is definitely interested in you like that."

And by the time either of us came up for air again, there wasn't a single doubt left in my mind.

CHAPTER 16

Ahmed

I woke up to warm skin pressed against mine.

It was such an unusual feeling, it disoriented me for a moment, but as I fluttered my eyes open, last night started to come back into focus.

Jason.

I was in bed with Jason.

He was cuddled next to me with an arm draped lazily over my stomach. Slow, soft breaths whispered across my neck, raising goose bumps all the way down my back, which was pressed perfectly against Jason's chest and stomach.

I smiled into the pillow as I closed my eyes again. Oh my God, this was perfect. And last night was real. That kiss at the carnival. Everything that happened once we were back at my apartment. It was like a dream. Or a fantasy I couldn't believe I'd never had before.

Jason. Kissing Jason. Sex with Jason.

It was all so mind-blowing and toe-curling—how had I never gone there before? Not even in my mind?

Oh. Right. Because I'd had a boyfriend up until very recently. Even while I was miserable, I didn't cheat. I didn't have a wandering eye. Yeah, I might've jerked off to thoughts of people besides Mark when I was extra frustrated—usually movie stars or whatever, someone I had no inkling about ever touching for real—but who didn't do that once in a while? Or maybe that had been a sign of how miserable I'd been with him. Whatever.

Point was, I didn't entertain ideas of actually hooking up with someone. And I sure as shit didn't catch a case of the feels for someone else.

But then Mark was gone, and Jason was there. Not "there" like jumping into bed with me, but "there" like making sure I was okay. Asking if I needed anything. Stepping up like the friend he was. He hadn't opportunistically slid into the space Mark had vacated—he'd just been exactly the friend he'd been for as long as I'd known him, and suddenly he'd been everything I wanted. Platonically. Affectionally. Sexually.

Romantically.

He hadn't snatched me up as soon as Mark had walked away. He'd just quietly been everything I could ever need or want until I'd opened my eyes and realized he was the man of my dreams.

Of course I love you. How could I not?

Behind me, Jason stirred a little. His lips brushed the back of my neck just beneath my hair, then curved into a grin when I arched against him. Sliding his hand up the middle of my chest and pulling himself closer to me, he murmured, "I didn't wake you up, did I?"

"Mmm, no. And that feels nice."

"What does?" He kissed that spot again. "This?"

"Mmhmm." I wriggled back against him.

Soft laughter warmed my shoulder, and the arm around

my waist tightened. I loved that. He wasn't possessive or restrictive—he was just holding me like it was the only thing in the world he wanted to do, and in that moment, it was the only thing in the world I wanted, too. I loved being touched. I loved being held. I didn't want to think about why I'd been so touch-starved after living with someone else for so long, so I just focused on basking in Jason's gentle affection. On enjoying this for as long as it lasted before he decided we'd been in bed long enough.

Except…Jason didn't seem to be in any hurry to get out of bed. We stayed like that for ages, curled together beneath the covers.

After a while, he loosened the arm around my stomach, and I was sure that meant the moment was over. Instead, he trailed the backs of his fingers up and down my arm. Then he ran them down my side and onto my hip. It wasn't a sexual gesture, for all it made my skin tingle—he was just… touching me.

As his hand drifted back to my stomach, then up to my chest, he skated his lips along the top of my shoulder. "I still can't believe we're doing this."

"Neither can I." I bit my lip as he kissed the side of my neck. "Kind of feels like we should've done it a long time ago."

"Can't be changed." He held me closer to him and murmured into my hair, "We're here now. You won't hear me complain."

I closed my eyes and wriggled back against him. I wouldn't complain about this either. Especially just cuddling and touching without trying to turn each other on. We'd get to that again—probably soon—but this? Oh God, this was perfect.

Perfect enough that I started to drift off again. For a while, I was still sure Jason would suddenly pull away and declare it was time to get up. I was braced for that sudden rush of cold air against skin that had been so comfortably warmed by his.

It didn't come. In fact, Jason wasn't the one to decide it was time for us to stop lounging in bed—the alarm on my phone did it instead.

"Oh, fuck." I groaned as I reached for it, which opened up some cool space between us and made me shiver. "We have to work today, don't we?"

"Goddammit." He waited until I'd shut off the alarm, then reeled me back in. Nuzzling into my neck, he murmured, "Five more minutes?"

I laughed softly as I closed my eyes, lightheaded from disbelief that someone actually wanted to stay in bed with me. "Five more minutes."

FIVE MORE MINUTES turned into ten more minutes, but we did finally get ourselves up and moving. Fortunately, I always set my alarm to give myself plenty of time to get to work in the morning, so we didn't have to rush. Not even after the shower—which we didn't delude ourselves into thinking was an attempt to save time or water—went on for...um...a while. We still made it to work on time, and we were both smiling thanks to an early morning orgasm apiece.

My smile didn't last long, though. After I'd seen a few patients, I ran into Lucas by the cluster of desks in the middle of the clinic, and my God, he looked like he hadn't slept in a month.

"Hey." Frowning, I cocked my head. "You okay?"

"Yeah. Yeah." He wiped a hand over his face and sighed. "Rough night."

I raised my eyebrows, not sure if I should press. Lucas and I were friends, but he was technically my boss, too, so the lines could get tricky to walk.

Leaning hard against an unoccupied desk, he said, "Tina's still getting headaches a lot. And she's just been…I don't know. Off?" He shook his head. "I'm worried about her."

Something prickled at the base of my spine, and the conversation I'd had last night with Jason echoed through my mind.

"Do you think…" I chewed my lip, second-guessing whether I should.

Lucas looked at me, his expression that of a man who was desperate for answers.

Shifting my weight, I quietly said, "Do you think she might be hiding, like…a drinking problem?"

He straightened. "A drinking—what? No! She never drinks. Ever."

"Not that any of us see, no."

The defensiveness and anger in his expression were impossible to miss, and I put up my hands before he started talking.

"I'm not making accusations, okay?" I kept my tone even. "But she's being evasive. She won't let you even try to figure out what's wrong. The headaches in the morning. Being—"

"I'd have seen it by now," he snapped. "And I'd be able to smell the liquor. We live together, for God's sake, so it's not like—"

"Then maybe I'm wrong!" I spread my palms. "Lucas, I'm not suggesting this to be flippant or—I'm worried about her, too."

His anger abated slightly.

I went on, "People get really good at hiding those things. It's not a weakness or obliviousness on your part if she succeeded."

Lucas's eyes lost focus. Slowly, his shoulders sank, and horror set into his expression as he leaned back against the desk again. "Do you…do you think she really has a problem?"

"I don't know," I whispered. "But maybe it's worth looking into."

He squeezed his eyes shut and rubbed his forehead with the heel of his hand. "It… Actually, it makes a lot of sense now that I think about it. She's been struggling with money, too—enough that it's made me worried about combining our finances—and… God. Planning the wedding has been stressing her into the ground. Maybe she's been…" He dropped his hand and looked at me. "Has she been drinking herself sick right in front of me and I didn't even see it?"

"It's not your fault," I told him gently. "If she does have a problem, she's trying really hard to hide it. She didn't *want* you to see it. She didn't want any of us to see it."

"But this is what I *do*," he protested. "I'm trained to—"

"And I'm trained to spot abuse cases, but it turns out I've been living with a verbally abusive and oppressive asshole for the last few years. Even now I can't quite bring myself to call it abuse because it was…" I shrugged heavily. "I mean, the point is that a lot of shit's way easier to spot from the outside. That's part of *why* we're trained to look for it."

Lucas blinked. Then he sighed. "I'm glad you finally saw it."

"I… Wait. You saw it too?"

He eyed me. "Are you kidding?" He pushed himself off the desk and fiddled with the edge of his tablet. "Mark was an asshole. And yeah, for the record, I *would* call it abuse."

I swallowed. "Yeah?"

"Are you kidding?" Lucas huffed sharply. "The way he had you walking on eggshells all the time? Giving you so much grief over every little thing that you'd panic if you even thought you'd left a light on or something? No, he never got physical with you, but Jesus, Ahmed. If what he did wasn't abuse, what the fuck was it?

I stared at him, and after a moment, I sighed. "Well, everyone apparently saw it but me." Sobering, I added a gentle, "And he didn't try nearly as hard to hide it as Tina might be hiding a drinking problem."

Lucas winced. "Yeah. True." He gave a dry, miserable laugh. "Fuck. Maybe that cartoon guy at the carnival saw something I didn't."

I pressed my lips together. Well, at least he'd said it so I didn't have to sound like I was losing my damn mind. I offered a non-committal, "Maybe?"

He blew out a breath. "I'll talk to her tonight. I should probably…" He nodded toward the exam rooms.

"Yeah, me too. I've got someone coming in to—"

"Hey, Ahmed?" Rachel appeared in the doorway dividing us from the reception area, a worried crease on her brow. "Someone's here to see you." The tightness of her lips and the slight dip of her chin added an unspoken *Get your ass out here and handle this.*

"Oh, that doesn't sound good." Lucas clapped my shoulder and hurried away to see his next patient.

I nodded at Rachel. "Coming." I told Kim I was stepping out for a sec and headed up front. It was probably that one pharmaceutical rep who was still salty that I wouldn't allow him to put up ads in our lobby. While we did more drug advertising than I would've liked, the doctors all put their foot down and only allowed medications that they personally thought were the best on the market to be promoted. This yoyo's meds were…not the best on the market.

Ugh. Fine. I rolled my eyes as I pushed open the door to the waiting area. I'd chase him out, just like I always—

I stopped dead.

Standing by the front desk, expression full of venomous fury, was my ex-goddamned-boyfriend.

Behind the desk, Rachel and the two receptionists were conspicuously trying to look anywhere but at either of us. All around the room, patients waited to be seen, including a few kids playing with some toys. Not the time or place for a confrontation, and Mark's expression *screamed* that he'd come here for exactly that.

Before he could say a word, I gestured for him to come back. We could do this in the hallway outside the clinic, but that was too out in the open. The less patients and colleagues heard, the better.

As he followed me into the back, he growled, "I knew you—"

"Stop." I faced him and stabbed a finger in his startled face as I hissed, "This is my *job*, Mark. Whatever you came here to say, it can wait until we're out of everyone else's earshot." Then I spun on my heel and stalked down the hall past my office and the exam rooms—I wanted to make sure we were *far* from any curious ears. My heart was pounding so hard I couldn't hear if he'd followed me, but when I stepped into the breakroom and turned around, he was there. Through my teeth, I said, "Shut the door."

He glared at me—he'd never liked me telling him what to do—but he closed the door.

"All right." I folded my arms across my scrubs. "What are you doing here?"

He narrowed his eyes. "You swore up and down you didn't cheat on me while we were together."

I jumped, startled by the accusation. "That's…because I didn't?"

"Uh-huh." Sarcasm dripped off his words. "And you weren't into that clown Jason, were you?" He stepped closer. "Sure didn't waste any time having him sleep over, did you?"

"Having him—" The wires connected, and fury spread through me like wildfire. "Okay, first? We're not together anymore, so who and what I do now is none of your fucking business. And second? How the hell do you *know*, Mark?"

"So you're not denying it," he said with a sneer.

I rolled my eyes, which was surprisingly liberating, given how many times I'd wanted to but hadn't dared to without waiting until his back was turned. God, I really had been under his thumb, hadn't I? It got the predictable result, too—his hackles went up and his eyes flashed with anger, but I spoke first: "I'm saying it's none of your business if I sucked every dick I could find the day after you moved out. I'm not yours, Mark. We're done. You ended this. You broke up with me. This is your decision, so—"

"And it turns out it was the right one," he snarled back. "Because that was *his* truck outside the apartment last night."

My skin crawled at the realization he'd come by sometime between when Jason and I got home and when we'd left for work. Oh fuck, the confrontation that would've ensued if we'd run into him? Holy shit.

"How do you know Jason's truck was there?" I demanded. "What were you doing outside my apartment?"

His lips pulled tight across his teeth. "Because I knew. I fucking knew that you wouldn't waste any goddamned time jumping into the sack with—"

"Stop. Stop right now." I put up my hands. "One, it's none of your business. Two, that's creepy as hell."

He just laughed sarcastically and rolled his eyes.

I was going to marry *you?*

In an instant, everything I'd said to Lucas was crystal clear and true. Everything about realizing in hindsight what an abusive, oppressive asshole I'd lived with. No, he'd never physically hurt me, but I'd had to navigate our entire relationship like it was a room full of tripwires and booby traps. All to keep *this* asshole from blowing a gasket over nothing?

What a fucking waste.

I stood straighter, tightening my arms across my chest. "Is that all you came to say? That you think I cheated on you with Jason because you're stalking me and saw his truck outside my apartment?"

His jaw worked. "I was right. That's all. You wanted him, and now you've got him. So don't say I was fucking wrong about—"

"You know what?" I shrugged as flippantly as I could. "Sure. Believe what you want. If it makes you feel better to think I've wanted Jason all this time, and that as soon as you bailed, I jumped into bed with him, then…fine. Knock your-self out." I pointed at the door. "But do it on your own time. We're done here."

"What? You can't just—"

"Yeah, I can." I brushed past him and pulled open the door. Gesturing for him to go through it, I said, "Walk out of here and don't ever come back. You so much as ruffle a paper on someone's desk or give someone a dirty look, I will call the cops. Drive a single *inch* into my apartment's parking lot, I will take out a restraining order. Do *not* test me, Mark."

Oh my God. Where was this spine when he and I were together? Because this felt *good*. Liberating. Long, long overdue.

It was even better when he swore under his breath, strode out of the room, and got the fuck out of my clinic.

I followed him until I was sure he was actually leaving, but I didn't go into the waiting area. Instead, I listened until the door closed. Then, safely hidden from view of any patients, I sagged against the wall and rubbed my temples.

Holy. Shit.

I should've done that years ago. Stood up to him. Told

him to fuck off. Kicked his ass out. Threatened to go scorched earth if he didn't leave. Now that he'd really shown what an asshole he was—stalking me? *really?*—I was even angrier at myself. I'd wasted so damn much time, and God only knew how much he'd fucked up my head, and—

"Ahmed?" Jason's voice snapped me out of my thoughts, and I looked up to see him watching me, gentle concern written all over his face. "You okay?"

I didn't even know the answer to that. Was I? Wasn't I? Because I was half walking on air and half wanting to curl up on the floor under the weight of all this wasted time. Did I want to celebrate? Or grieve? No fucking idea.

And Jason...

He stepped across the space between us and wrapped his arms around me.

Closing my eyes, I leaned into his embrace. We'd hugged plenty of times in the past, but after last night, his body was even more familiar against mine. That didn't turn me on this time—it sent relief rushing through me. Hell, it almost made me break down right there on his shoulder.

Yeah, I'd wasted a lot of years under Mark's thumb, but when I'd finally stepped out into the light, there was Jason. Sweet. Kind. Loving. No questions. No judgment. He didn't give me any grief for staying with Mark for so long—he just took my hand, led me all the way out into the sun, and held me like I hadn't been held *once* in the last five years.

After a long moment, Jason whispered, "Want me to kick his ass?"

Laughter poured out of me so suddenly I almost swayed. As I drew back to meet his gaze, I said, "Nah. Wouldn't do me any good to have you go to jail right when I finally started dating you."

Oh, that blush. My God, how did I never notice how adorable Jason was?

"Well, I mean…" With a sheepish expression, he slipped his hands into the pockets of his scrub pants. "I could do it without getting caught."

I chuckled and rolled my eyes, which finally got a mischievous snicker out of him.

I rested my hands on his chest. "Thank you." Because we both knew what he was doing—trying to make me laugh when I was obviously upset. And he'd succeeded, because he always did, because he always seemed to know exactly what I needed to hear.

No, it wasn't that—he cared enough to figure it out.

He touched my face, running his thumb along the edge of my beard. "Seriously, though, you good? I didn't hear what went on, but you guys didn't look happy."

"I'm fine." I covered his hand with mine and squeezed gently. "I really am."

He smiled, the relief unmistakable. "Okay. Just say so if—"

"Hey, Ahmed?" Rachel appeared in the doorway. "Can you —oh." Her jaw went slack. Jason and I had quickly separated upon hearing her voice, but probably not fast enough for her to miss the way we'd been touching. She blinked a couple of times, then smiled and rolled her eyes. "Well, that was inevitable. Anyway, you've both got patients. Check your tablets—we're starting to fall behind."

"Right. On it." I cleared my throat. "Thanks."

She gave us both an amused look before disappearing into the reception area again.

"Well." Jason chuckled as we both headed back toward his desk and my office. "Guess we don't need to come out to the staff."

"No, probably not." I hesitated, slowing to a stop just outside my office. "Is that… Are you okay with that? With people knowing?"

The smile on his face made my knees weak. "Am I okay

with people knowing I'm with you? Are you kidding me?" He motioned back toward where Rachel was working. "I was going to ask if she'd get 'Ahmed's Boyfriend' embroidered on my next set of scrubs."

I laughed and rolled my eyes, and he chuckled too.

"Okay." I stepped closer and lifted my chin to suggest a kiss. "Then I guess we won't hide."

Jason grinned. Then he kissed me.

Just lightly and quickly—we were at work, after all, and we needed to get back to it—but enough that if anyone caught a glimpse of us, there'd be no mistaking that we were more than colleagues or friends.

As I headed back to my office to get my tablet and resume seeing patients, I couldn't stop smiling. The encounter with Mark had sucked, but it was worth it for the clarity, and for the moment after with Jason.

Mark and I were over. What he thought of me and what he told other people—I didn't care. It didn't matter.

I was out from under his thumb. It was done.

And by some miracle, my best friend wanted me.

CHAPTER 17

Jason

W e ended up back at the carnival that night.

As we'd crossed paths throughout the day and had lunch together, we'd batted around a few ideas for what to do that evening. It was a Friday night, so neither of us had to work tomorrow, and this would more or less count as our first date. There were plenty of options, from going out for dinner and a movie to hanging out at his place for the same.

"I'm game for anything," he'd pointed out with a grin. *"Especially since I'm pretty sure I know where we'll be at the end of the night."*

Fuck. Was it quitting time yet?

At some point, we'd landed on the idea of going back to the carnival. This would be our fourth trip, but we were going with a different mission this time. Or rather, with the same mission we'd had the first time—to enjoy ourselves and the carnival atmosphere. We just wouldn't have our friends or his dipshit ex with us this time.

No hunting down the button game. No worrying about the painting. No trying not to set off Mark's temper.

Just me, Ahmed, and the carnival.

"I'm still going to keep it in my bag." Ahmed pulled his backpack out from behind the passenger seat in my truck. "Just in case."

I feigned offense as I came around the front. "What? You don't think your bad luck has come to a spectacular end?" I gestured dramatically at myself.

He made a show of looking me up and down, pursing his lips as if he were giving it some serious thought. "Okay, you have a point." He shrugged the pack onto his shoulders. "But just in case."

"Uh-huh." I hooked a finger in his belt loop and tugged him toward me. "You just think it's turned into a good luck charm all of a sudden, and you want to see what else it gets you." I pulled him in close enough that our lips were almost touching. "Sorry, baby. This is the jackpot. It doesn't get any better than this."

Then I closed the rest of the distance, muffling his laugh with my lips, and he wrapped his arms around my neck as he leaned into me. It had been less than twenty-four hours since our first kiss, and I'd already decided this was one of my favorite things ever—making him laugh right before I kissed him. There was something so exhilarating about getting that reaction out of him, and then feeling his lips curve against mine before they softened into a kiss.

"We should get our tickets," he murmured. "Or we're just going to end up in the bed of your truck."

"You say that like it's a bad thing."

Ahmed chuckled as he drew back. "We'll get to that part." He winked and took my hand. "But we came all the way out here, so..." He nodded toward the carnival entrance and raised his eyebrows.

As if I could say no.

Sure, it was fun to imagine seizing every chance we could to fool around, but I liked this part, too. I'd also had to walk on eggshells because of Mark, even if it was to a lesser extent, and now Ahmed and I could be relaxed and open with each other. As both friends and more than friends.

Sex could wait while we spent some time just being together.

After we'd bought our tickets, we strolled around the carnival. No mission. No stress. It didn't even bother me that we had that cursed thing with us.

"Is it weird that I feel like the curse is actually gone?" I asked as we wandered past the carousel. "Like, there seemed to be bullshit falling out of the sky, and then it kind of…stopped."

"I've noticed that, too." Ahmed paused. "Actually…maybe that's not quite right."

"How do you figure?"

"Well, it's not so much that I feel like the bad luck is magi-cally gone." He gave my hand a gentle squeeze. "Just…seems like whatever comes will be a lot easier to face now."

Oh, the things this man did to my heart.

My cheeks heated, and I pretended not to notice as I grinned. "See? I told you! You hit the good-luck jackpot, and now—"

"Oh, shut up," he laughed, and elbowed me playfully.

"What? I'm just saying."

"Uh-huh. Have I ever told you what a brat you are?"

"I can be more of one."

"You don't have to tell me." He shot me a challenging look. "I can be one, too."

"Mmhmm, yes, but I have one thing you don't."

His eyebrow arched.

I held up the truck keys and jingled them.

"Oh, that's just cold." Then he smirked. "But if you make me walk home, then it's you and your hand tonight, isn't it?"

I scowled.

"Ha!" He nudged me with his shoulder. "Now who's the brat?"

"Still me." I brought his hand up and kissed the back of it. "But it's cute that you tried."

Ahmed scoffed. "Ugh. Fine."

We exchanged playful glares and kept walking, my fingers still laced between his. I was cautious about being affectionate in public with another man, but I'd kissed Ahmed right in the middle of this carnival and no one had even seemed to notice. Walking around with his hand in mine didn't feel nearly as reckless as it should have, and I basked in it—not just being demonstrative with a man, but with Ahmed. Because somehow...by some ridiculous miracle or the planets aligning or something...I'd woken up in his bed this morning. He was with me now. On an actual date. Holding my hand like there'd never been any reason not to.

I wondered how long it would take for this to start feeling real.

Abruptly, Ahmed halted, and I nearly stumbled beside him. "What?"

He stared past me, his jaw slack and his eyes huge. I followed the trajectory of his gaze and—

"Are you fucking kidding me?" I breathed.

Buttons of Mystery, the hand-painted sign announced. *A game for young and old! Find the secret—win a prize!*

Tucked in between a couple of booths I knew for a fact we'd seen on all of our visits—including a game we'd played a few times, both with our friends and on our own—there it fucking was.

Same three old barrels with people pawing around in

buttons. Same mustached guy with a silver pocket watch attached to his waistcoat. Same rows of prizes up on the wall.

"I'm not hallucinating, am I?" Ahmed sounded dazed. "That's…that's the game, right?"

"Uh-huh." I shook myself and blinked a few times, but the game was still there. I could even hear the rattle of buttons as people raked their fingers through them, the sound tickling that memory of the shortbread tin in Grandma's sewing room. "We walked by here a million times, though. I know we did."

Ahmed nodded slowly. "No kidding. And the girl from the dart booth—I lost her right…" He looked around. "Right over there." He gestured at another booth, one where we'd stopped to gather our bearings after yet another guide had been waylaid.

"I am so confused right now," I said.

"Me too." Ahmed swung the backpack down onto his elbow. "But now that we found it…"

"Good call. Let's go."

We marched across the thin flow of fairway traffic, and I never took my eyes off that booth. I was sure it was going to vanish if I did.

It didn't, though. When we reached the other side of the well-packed dirt, the booth and the man with the pocket watch were still there.

We waited while the man finished up with the people playing. Then he turned to us. "Step right up and—oh! I remember you gentlemen!" He grinned. "Did you come to try again?" He made a sweeping gesture at the barrels.

I was…admittedly…tempted.

My fingers itched with the urge to run through those buttons, but I occupied them by wrapping my arm around Ahmed's shoulders.

Subtly, maybe even unconsciously, he shifted his weight to lean into me. I loved that.

"We don't want to play this time," he said, opening up his backpack. "But I wanted to bring this back." He pulled out the painting and offered it to the man.

The man regarded it, then us. "Bring it back? Don't you like it?"

"No, I do," Ahmed said apologetically. "But I swear, I've had the worst luck since I got it. And I'm, uh, sorry it's kind of dirty. I tried to clean it up a bit, but—"

"It looks fine to me." The man gently took it from his hands and turned it, inspecting it in the light from the incandescent bulbs strung up over our heads. "Just the way I gave it to you!"

The fuck? It was covered in soot and dried nacho cheese, not to mention some grease from my toolkit and the spots where the "potion" had splattered on it, so it—

Wait.

No.

All of that was gone.

Even the spots where the potion had desaturated the colors were gone, leaving behind the slightly faded but otherwise undisturbed paintjob.

Ahmed looked at me, brow furrowed. "You saw it, didn't you?"

I nodded. "Yeah, I definitely did."

"Well." The man smiled as he pulled the drab green ammunition box from under a table. "It looks fine to me. If you're sure you don't want to keep it..." He held it up like he was about to slot the picture in with the others, a questioning expression on his face.

"I'm sure," Ahmed said, absently wrapping his arm around my waist. "Like I said...bad luck. Or something." He laughed self-consciously. "I'll feel better with it gone."

The man studied us. He looked at me. Looked at Ahmed. Let his eyes drift to Ahmed's hand on my side and my hand on his shoulder. Then an odd little smile curled up beneath his mustache, and as he tucked the painting into the box, he said, "I don't think it's bad luck. But I do think it did what it was meant to do." He shut the lid and latched it. "I'll hold on to it for the next person."

"What it was meant to do?" I asked. "What do you mean?"

He just smiled.

Right then, some teenagers came up, waving tickets and asking if they could play the game. The operator gave us a nod before turning his attention to his next customers. Ahmed and I exchanged glances, shrugged, and walked away.

"I feel kind of stupid about it now," Ahmed said. "But… I'm also glad it's gone."

"Let's just hope it stays gone this time."

Beneath my arm, Ahmed shuddered. "Yeah. Let's hope."

"If it does, I say we buy lottery tickets."

Ahmed laughed. "Deal."

I chuckled, and we continued walking. Just before we turned the corner at the end of the row, I glanced back the way we'd come.

Everything was exactly as we left it. The games. The crowd. The noise.

But there was no sign of *Buttons of Mystery*.

CHAPTER 18

Ahmed

*I*t was a little after eleven when we finally meandered out to the parking lot. The carnival was showing no signs of slowing down, though I had no idea how late it actually ran, but we were both ready to call it a night. We'd walked every inch of this place on our previous three visits and again tonight, and this evening we'd played enough games, ridden enough rides, and eaten enough food that we'd both be budgeting carefully until payday.

No regrets. The night was absolutely perfect. And as first dates went, it didn't get any better than this. We weren't a couple of strangers meeting up after a few Tinder conversations. We knew each other. We were comfortable with each other. It seemed crass to call our relationship "friends with benefits," but in a way, it kind of was. Not because we were friends who fucked for the hell of it. We were just…friends who'd taken things to a new level. We had this amazing friendship, and now we'd added to it. Sex, yes, but so much more than that. It was like we'd taken the long way to love by being friends first, and once we got here, it was effortless. It made perfect sense to touch and kiss. We knew each other's quirks. We could read each other's tells and course correct if we brushed up against a boundary.

I had no illusions that a relationship would be free of any kind of bumps or conflicts. Hell, we'd had plenty of arguments as friends and colleagues. I just knew we could work it out because...we had. Multiple times. A relationship with him wouldn't be perfect, just like it wouldn't be with anyone else. But it would be perfect for me. And hopefully for him.

Tonight seemed like a pretty good start.

Lacing our fingers together on the way out, I said, "Thank you for this. Coming out here with me again."

That smile was going to be the death of me. Seriously.

"Thank *you*," he said. "I had a great time."

"Me too."

He flashed me another smile, and we kept walking toward the truck.

We were almost there when Jason suddenly halted. "Oh. Wow."

"Hmm?" I turned to him, and I realized he was staring upward. When I did the same... Yeah. Wow.

Despite the bright lights of the carnival, the sky was dusted with thousands of stars. It was the kind of view I'd only seen out in the desert or way out in a rural area with no light pollution. Where we were now would've usually qualified, and somehow the carnival wasn't dimming the spectacular view.

"That's gorgeous," I whispered, as if speaking too loudly would scatter all the stars.

"It really is. Do you—" Jason cut himself off, and when I looked at him again, he was biting his lip.

I squeezed his hand and gently prodded, "Do I...?"

He swallowed. After a moment, he faced me. "I've got a couple of blankets in the truck. Want to chill in the bed and..." He gestured skyward.

My heart did things it never had before. Lie on some blankets and watch the stars? With Jason?

"Yeah," I breathed. "Yeah, let's. That sounds amazing."

Jason's face lit up brighter than the stars or the carnival. "Great! Let me get the blankets out."

We continued toward his truck, and I climbed into the bed while he reached behind the seats to retrieve the blankets. Two were thick, ugly moving blankets—those weird blue padded things people used to wrap furniture. The third was fuzzy orange with a familiar logo on it.

I eyed him. "Did you steal these from U-Haul?"

"I didn't steal them." He hoisted himself up into the bed. "I just...forgot to return them."

"Uh-huh."

He met me with a challenging look. "You want to use my shamelessly stolen blankets? Or lie right on the metal?" He tapped his sneaker against the bed we were standing on.

I pursed my lips. "So, which one goes down first?

He laughed. "That's what I thought."

We settled on top of the two moving blankets with the incriminating U-Haul blanket rolled up like a pillow, and we stared up at the beautiful sky. Truthfully, though, I barely noticed the stars once I was beside him. Lying against him like this felt good. It felt like the most natural thing in the world. I'd rocketed right past disbelieving we were doing this to wondering how in hell it had taken me so long to realize this was where I belonged.

Some time passed. Half an hour, maybe? I lost track.

Then Jason broke the silence. "I'm not saying this because

we're dating now, but…" He turned toward me and stroked my hair. "I just have to say, I'm really glad you're not with Mark anymore."

The comment caught me off-guard, and I laughed. "You seriously didn't like him, did you?"

"It's not that I didn't like Mark." He paused. "Okay, I didn't. Never did. He was…" Jason waved a hand. "The point is, what I disliked about him the most was how he treated you."

My laughter was gone, though I was still startled. "Really?"

"Are you kidding?" His palm warmed my cheek. "No one deserves that. But it pissed me off to no end to see someone treating *you* that way. I didn't care if you ended up with me or anyone else as long as they treated you right."

I had no idea what to say to that, and I wasn't even sure my voice would hold if I tried. With some effort, I managed, "It bothered you that much?"

"Of course it did." He carded his fingers through my hair. "You're my friend. I want you to be happy."

At that, I smiled, and I slid my hand up his forearm. "I am now. Not just because I'm done with him, but because I'm with you."

He returned the smile and leaned in for a kiss. It was a light one—not the kind that would have us spun up and looking for someplace private—but it made my spine tingle just the same.

After a moment, he drew back, and he took a breath like he was about to say something, but he hesitated. Then he dropped his gaze and chewed his lip.

"What's on your mind?" I asked.

"I just…" He sighed. "I don't know what counts as moving too fast with something like this. Like where the timer starts for certain things, you know?"

I furrowed my brow, because no, I didn't know. Though I did *kind* of follow. "Because we just sort of sidestepped into a relationship instead of going through the motions that everyone else does."

Jason nodded, avoiding my eyes. "Exactly. So it's hard to tell what..." He trailed off with a frustrated sigh.

I closed my hand around his. "Jason. We're friends. We get to skip that stage where everything is fragile and we have to be on our best behavior or be super careful what we say and do." I shrugged. "If something is too fast, we can always tap the brakes, you know? It doesn't have to be a dealbreaker."

He chewed his lip, still not looking at me.

Concern roiled in the pit of my stomach. I never liked seeing someone I cared about upset or uncomfortable, but this was Jason being worried—hell, freaked out—about me. I didn't like that at all.

"Talk to me," I whispered. "Whatever it is, we can do more about it out in the open than you worrying yourself sick over it."

He looked at me through those long lashes, studying me uncertainly.

"Talk to me," I repeated gently. "It's me, Jason. Not some guy who's going to bolt if you break some unwritten rule of dating."

That got a small laugh out of him. Then he sobered, and he swallowed hard. Reaching for my face, he whispered, "We just started doing this." His fingertips landed gently on my cheek, sending all kinds of electricity through my body, and I had to fight the urge to move in closer. Jason moistened his lips. "And even after everything I said last night, I'm still afraid it's too soon to tell you I love you."

Oh. God. The things going on in my chest right then. I couldn't remember the last time I'd heard those words from anyone outside my family, and to hear them from him—a shaky, nervous whisper from my best friend, terrified he was going to scare me off even though he'd already told me he was in love with me—made a million different emotions tumble through me at once.

He winced, averting his gaze, and I could hear the *"I'm sorry"* coming before he'd even pulled in a breath.

I stopped those words with a kiss.

He stiffened at first, but slowly, that tension eased, and when his hand slid up into my hair, I was surprised I didn't cry from relief and joy and so much love.

It was almost painful to break that kiss, but I did so I could shakily whisper, "I love you, too."

The surprise in his expression would've been comical under any other circumstances. "You…you do?"

"Of course I do." I cupped the back of his neck and dusted another kiss across his parted lips. "It feels like this thing we're doing is too new for that, you know? But also…it isn't. It's like it's about damn time, you know? We just started dating last night, but this"—I gestured at him and myself—"didn't just fall out of the sky, you know? We've been friends for ages. I loved you like that all along, and I knew it." I traced the edge of his jaw with the pad of my thumb. "I just didn't realize I'd completely fallen for you too."

The utter bewilderment on his face was adorable. So was the smile that slowly came to life. He didn't say a word, though—just drew me in and kissed me, and that long, gentle kiss said it all.

Of course I loved him. Of course we'd made it to this. Where else would I have ever landed but in his arms?

At the edges of my senses, I was aware of the carnival still going on. The vibrations of the rides were almost palpable from here, and the music danced along my nerve endings like a conversation I could *just* hear, but couldn't make out the words.

The carnival. This whole debacle that had kept us coming back to this field, over and over, in search of something we'd finally found, and it had landed us…here.

I lifted my head and grinned at him. "I guess that love potion worked after all."

"Nah." Jason traced the edge of my beard with his fingertip. "I don't think it did."

I tilted my head. "You don't?"

"No." His hand drifted up into my hair. "I loved you long before Peyton bought that bottle."

My heart fluttered. Didn't matter how many times he told me he'd loved me for so long—it would still make me weak in the knees.

"Okay, so *you* didn't need it," I whispered. "But maybe I did."

His brow furrowed.

I pulled back a little more so we could see each other without going cross-eyed. "It's not that I needed it to fall for you. I think I've been there for a long time." I laced our fingers together. "But it kind of seems like that and the painting—I don't know. It's like they pushed over some dominos that needed to fall so we could end up here. Maybe that means, in a roundabout way that makes a lot more sense in hindsight…they worked."

He pursed his lips and seemed to think about that for a few seconds. Then he smiled and stroked fingers across my cheek. "I won't argue with the process if this is the end result."

"Neither will I." Even as I said it, though, worry clouded my thoughts. What if this thing between us got lopsided? I'd spent a long time hearing that I wasn't worth a damn as a partner; what if there was truth to that? What if Jason got tired of—

"Hey." He lifted my chin so I had to meet his concerned eyes. "Where'd you go?"

I swallowed. "Just…" I chewed my lip. "I've been so dependent on you. As a friend."

Surprise lifted his eyebrows. "What do you mean?"

"Like…" I thought about it, and I stared down at our hands as I said, "Whenever I have a crisis, or I'm upset, or—just, any time there's something wrong, you're the first person I go to. You always drop everything for me. No question." I caressed his cheek. "And I know you're the reason my workload was lighter the day after Mark and I split up."

The blush and the way he shyly avoided my gaze confirmed what I'd already pieced together.

I squeezed his hand. "You're always keeping me upright. I'm so damn needy, and—"

"Ahmed." He ran his thumb along my bottom lip. "I care about you." A gentle smile lifted the corners of his mouth. "I love you. Whether you're my friend or my boyfriend, I want to be there for you like that."

God, the things this man did to my heart.

"But I feel like I take advantage of that. I call you for everything, and lean on you for—"

He kissed me softly, stopping my protests with his lips, and what could I do but melt in the warmth of his gentle touch and his perfect kiss? Especially when he was trying to reassure me that I wasn't too much for him?

How did I not realize how much I loved you before now?

When he drew back, he whispered, "You're not taking advantage of anything. You've never asked more than I'm willing to give. And you do the same for me all the time." He laughed softly, his breath gusting across my lips. "You think it's imbalanced in your favor—I wonder all the time if it's the opposite."

I pulled away enough to see his face, and I held his gaze. "You do?"

"All the time." He ran his fingers through my hair. "You've needed a lot lately because you've had a lot thrown at you. So it probably seems to you like you're asking too much. But you've been amazing the whole time I've known you. You went with me to my friend's funeral so I didn't have to go alone, even though we both knew you needed to be studying for your board. You were my biggest support when Daniel and I split up. You're…" He laughed softly, shaking his head. "If you could see our friendship from my point-of-view, you'd never question that things are lopsided in your favor."

My mouth had gone dry. I had no idea what to say.

"And it's not just with me," he went on. "Ahmed, you're the most selfless person I've ever known. For *everyone* around you. Friends. Family. Patients. Colleagues. Total strangers." He half-shrugged. "I've seen you bend over backwards for people when it's obvious you're already at your own breaking point." He looked right in my eyes, his expression and his voice so full of sincerity it made my heart ache: "If I can be there to keep you afloat while you're keeping everyone else afloat, then that sounds perfect to me."

"You're amazing," I whispered.

"Nah." His lopsided little grin was too cute for words. "Just the luckiest guy in the world."

I laughed softly and kissed him. "We'll see how you feel after dating me for a while."

"I've been your friend and coworker for three years. I know exactly how much of a pain in the ass you are."

I snorted. "Is that going to be on my Valentine's Day card?"

"Probably."

Rolling my eyes, I leaned in again for a kiss. This still blew my mind. Despite—or somehow because of—a few days of the worst luck I'd ever experienced in my life, I had the best boyfriend I could ever ask for.

"In all seriousness," I whispered. "I love you, Jason. I can't believe I didn't realize that sooner."

"I think this is the perfect time." He kissed me softly, breaking it for only a second to murmur, "I love you so much."

I didn't think I'd ever get tired of hearing him say that.

Just like I couldn't imagine ever getting tired of how much his kiss turned me on. How much his hands on my body made me want to get us both out of our clothes and into a sweat.

"Why does home have to be so far away?" I grumbled between kisses.

Jason laughed. "What do you mean?"

I slid my hand up his back, tugging at his shirt. "Because that's a lot of miles between us and a place where we can get naked."

His breath hitched and he shivered against me. Skating his lips down my neck, he murmured, "I mean, we're technically in a bed."

A laugh burst out of me. "We're also out in public."

Jason shrugged. Then he met my gaze and grinned. "So we don't get completely naked and we don't fuck." He glanced around, shrugged again, and looked down at me. "But I'm pretty sure I can do something about…" He rutted against my hard-on, driving a frustrated moan out of me.

Fuck it. I wanted him. No way in hell was I going to make it back to the apartment before I did something about his hard-on and mine.

I paused for a quick glance around the truck to make sure we were alone. Then, sliding a hand between us, I cupped his dick and squeezed just enough to make him moan. "I'm in."

His eyes flew open, the lights from the carnival illuminating the unmistakable heat in his gaze. "Yeah?"

"Mmhmm."

He looked startled for a moment, but then he grinned.

And as he came back in to kiss me, he growled, "Game on."

CHAPTER 19

Jason

*S*omewhere in the back of my mind, I was pretty sure I should've been thinking about that stupid button game, and how it had reappeared and then disappeared. About the cryptic comments from the man running it. About the painting that shouldn't have been that pristine when Ahmed pulled it out of his backpack tonight.

That was all weird as hell and should've been occupying every brain cell that wasn't busy operating some necessary organ.

But it was about as close to the forefront of my mind as the distant noise and music of the carnival, because nothing about that game or the painting held a candle to how unreal the scene was in the back of my truck.

Ahmed. In my arms. Kissing me. Wanting me. Loving me.

This was happening? It was real?

Yes. It was. And every brush of his lips or fingers, every whisper of his breath across my skin, every moan shaped like my name—it blew my mind. Every one. Every time. One miracle after another. Maybe that sounded melodramatic, but I'd spent three years convincing myself this man would never have a flicker of interest in me and that he'd never get away from that jackwagon who didn't deserve him. Having him in my arms like this mere days after Mark had exited stage left? Yeah, that felt fucking miraculous to me, and I mentally celebrated every time Ahmed touched me, kissed me, murmured that he wanted me.

And he'd said he loved me.

Oh my God, he loved me.

I buried my face in his neck to compose myself, hiding the sudden rush of emotion with kisses all along the side of his throat. Ahmed dragged his hands up my back as he murmured, "Fuck, I love that."

"Yeah?" I trailed more kisses up to the underside of his jaw, right to the edge of his beard.

Ahmed just moaned, digging his nails into my back. He squirmed under me, then managed to say, "Tell me what you want."

As if I didn't have everything I could ever ask for right now, but...I knew what he meant.

"I want to suck you off." I paused to nip his earlobe. "I want you to come in my mouth."

The sound he made—the throaty, helpless moan—almost did me in. He was out of breath when he asked, "Yeah? That's what you want?" He sounded disbelieving.

"Uh-huh." I came up and brushed my lips across his. "I love giving head. Especially finishing."

His eyes widened a little. Then he grinned. "Don't let me stop you." The grin faltered. "I...guess I did stop you last night, but—"

"Are you kidding? That was hot as hell."

"Was it?"

I cocked a brow. "You begging me to kiss you and then

coming while we made out? Uh, yes. Yes, 'hot' is the word I would use to describe that."

Ahmed laughed, almost masking the relief. Jesus, he really wasn't used to someone who wanted to make him happy, was he?

"Get used to this," I said softly, smoothing his hair. "There's nothing in the world that turns me on more than driving my partner out of his mind."

He bit his lip. "Same."

"So we understand each other?"

He slid a hand into my back pocket and squeezed my ass. "We understand each other."

There was no holding back anymore. We made out until we were both out of breath, and I kept on kissing him while I undid his pants, just so I could catch all those little gasps and moans as I freed his dick. A few strokes had him cursing between kisses and rutting into my hand, and my own cock was straining against my zipper because holy fuck, this man turned me on.

Ahmed writhed under me, rocking himself into my fist as if he were desperate for friction. "God, your mouth is amazing. I want you to… *Please*."

I kissed him, murmured an affirmative, and then moved down. The instant my tongue touched his cock, Ahmed released a ragged breath and shuddered from head to toe. "Fuuuck."

"Like that?"

"Uh-huh. Seriously, your mouth is—oh, Jesus…"

I would've grinned at his reaction had I not been taking him deep into my throat right then. I fucking loved this. Turning him on. Driving him wild. I didn't care how long it had taken us to get here, only that we finally had, and that it was worth every second of pining frustration to be the one making him whimper and tremble now. Tonight, I'd make him come like this, and then we had all the time in the world to learn every imaginable way to satisfy each other.

Shame this carnival didn't have a website, because I'd have left it the most glowing review *ever*.

Ahmed tensed, and my thoughts scattered as he went completely still and silent. For a split second, I worried I'd done something wrong, but then I caught on—there were voices and footsteps coming closer. Nothing about them indicated they knew two guys were fooling around in this truck, but if someone decided to crane their neck over the siderails…

Moving as stealthily as I could, I came back up beside Ahmed, pulling the blanket over us in hopes of being in a somewhat less compromising position if we got caught.

We stayed stock still and dead silent, listening as relaxed laughter and chatter drew closer, punctuated by the crunch of shoes on gravel. A few heads bobbed past, just far enough away that they wouldn't catch us out of the corners of their eyes. As long as no one turned an absentmindedly curious glance into the truck bed, we'd be fine.

No one looked. The group passed by, preoccupied by their conversations and oblivious to us.

They didn't get far, though. Maybe twenty, thirty feet away if I had to guess, the footsteps stopped. The conversations, however, did not.

Voices carried as they lingered like my friends and I sometimes did when the party was over but we weren't quite ready to leave. Laughter. Teasing someone about his poor performance on a game. Ranting about how another game was definitely rigged. I heard a car door open and close, but only one, and no engines started up.

"Are you fucking kidding me?" Ahmed grumbled near-silently. "Just…*go!*"

I pressed my face into his shoulder to muffle a laugh.

"Maybe this was a bad idea," he muttered. "I'm hard as a goddamned rock, but—"

"You don't think I can finish you off?"

He twisted to look at me, his expression full of horror. "There's people, like…" He flailed his hand. "Right there!"

"Mmhmm. Excellent observation." I grinned. "You'll just have to be quiet."

"Jason," he warned.

"Have to be quiet." I kissed him, then started down his neck. "Absolutely quiet."

Ahmed stifled a frustrated groan and whispered, "You are such an asshole."

"Are you saying no?"

He squirmed under me. "I'm saying you better get your mouth back on my dick before I come all over your shirt."

I laughed and kissed his collarbone. "That's what I thought."

Then I did exactly what I was told, and Ahmed barely made a sound, though his whole body was immediately wound tight, arching and wriggling as I licked up and down his shaft. Those near-silent gasps, the way his fingers curled painfully in my hair—it was so damn sexy. Could I make him come like this? Drive him wild without letting him make a sound? Because that would be hot as hell.

Nearby, the conversations took on the sound of people saying goodbye to each other, calling across increasing distances about "See you later" and "Thanks for coming." Car doors started opening and closing. An engine turned over. Then another. Soon, there were no sounds near us except for a few vehicles making their way down the gravel road.

"Oh, thank fuck," Ahmed groaned, arching off the truck bed and pushing his dick into my mouth. "*God*, that's good."

I moaned around him, which made him shudder and squirm some more. He dragged his fingers through my hair, pulling just hard enough to sting, and every sound he made had me closer to losing my own mind. I finally couldn't take it anymore, and I shifted onto one arm while I undid my jeans. Then I was blowing him for all I was worth while I pumped myself, driven higher and higher by his moans and gasps, not to mention his hard dick in my mouth and the friction of my own hand. It limited how much I could use my hand on him, but he didn't seem to mind at all.

"You gonna come too?" he panted. "Oh my God, Jason. That's… Fuck, that's hot."

I moaned again, going to town on both of us, and Ahmed peppered the air with whispered curses and sharp gasps. The truck's suspension gave a couple of halfhearted creaks that would probably give us away if anyone walked by, but…fuck it. I was too turned on, too ready to swallow his cum and go off myself, and Ahmed didn't sound the least bit worried about us getting busted.

He sucked in a breath and managed, "Gonna come," a second before his hips bucked off the truck bed and he unloaded across my tongue. I just managed to swallow every drop before I was coming too, and I had to lift off him so I could groan, "Oh, *fuck*," as I came on my hand.

"Holy shit," he slurred. "That was hot."

"Uh-huh. It was."

Lifting himself up on an elbow as I came back up to join him, he grinned. "Next time, it's my turn."

"Oh yeah?" I returned the grin and kissed him lightly. "You won't hear any objections from me."

"Figured I wouldn't."

We both chuckled and shared another lazy kiss.

I found some shop towels stashed in my toolbox off to the side of the bed, and after I'd cleaned my hand and the few stray drops that had landed on our clothes, I lay beside Ahmed again.

All around us, people were heading back to their cars.

In the distance, the carnival still clattered on.

Above us, the stars still glowed brilliantly against an ink-black sky.

Somehow, it was all even more vivid and bright than before, as if my senses were all hypersensitive after giving us each an orgasm. I was a little sex-drowsy too, but I didn't think I was in any danger of falling asleep.

Everything was just…perfect.

Ahmed settled with his head on my chest. "You know, I gotta say—a blowjob in the bed of a truck in a carnival parking lot is definitely a new experience."

I cracked up, and he vibrated against me with quiet amusement. "I'm sure we can come up with equally classy places for dates. The Walmart parking lot, maybe?"

He snickered. "Oh, come on. We can do better than that."

"Hmm. Lowe's? Target?"

"Ooh, now you're talking." He cuddled closer to me. "Make it Dick's, and I'm yours forever."

That had us both laughing harder. Christ, this was perfect. Hot sex. Easy banter. We really had just upgraded our amazing friendship, hadn't we? Best. Relationship. Ever.

We stared up at the stars for a while, neither of us moving or speaking. Eventually, Ahmed asked, "Should we head back?" He sounded disappointed by his own suggestion.

"Probably." I stroked his hair. "But I kind of don't want to move yet."

"Mmm, same." He cuddled closer to me, draping his arm across my stomach. "I don't mind staying for a little while."

"Isn't like we have to get up for work tomorrow."

"That's true."

"So…a little while longer?"

"A little while longer."

I smiled and kissed his temple.

Lying there in the bed of my truck with Ahmed's head on my shoulder, serenaded by sounds of the carnival as we stared up at the stars, I was in no hurry to go anywhere.

Right here, right now...

My world was perfect.

MY EYELIDS FLUTTERED OPEN, and for a few panicked seconds, I didn't know where I was.

Outdoors, definitely. Bathed in the steadily warming gray light of dawn. Covered in a blanket with...

Ahmed.

As soon as I caught on that he was against me, his arm draped over me and his head on my shoulder, everything snapped into focus.

Well, almost everything. I remembered us lying here and staring up at the stars, but had we actually fallen asleep? And stayed here all night? Apparently so, because the sun was definitely coming up.

Shit. Good thing we didn't have to go to work today.

I shifted a little, trying to stretch some sore muscles without disturbing Ahmed. I failed at both—my whole body was stiff from sleeping on this hard surface, and Ahmed stirred.

"Hey," I said, my voice raspy from sleep.

"Hey." He glanced up at me, that adorably sleepy smile on his face. He started to say something, but then looked up, squinted, and glanced around. His body tensed. "Where the hell..."

"We fell asleep in the truck."

"In the—" He blinked. "Shit, we never left the carnival?"

I shook my head and laughed. "Guess not."

"Well, damn." He wiped a hand over his face, skin hissing over his beard. "Good thing they didn't charge us by the hour."

"I know, right?" I twisted a crick out of my back, but didn't get up. "Eh, I've slept in worse places."

"Me too." His face took on a distant expression.

"You okay?" I asked.

"Yeah, yeah. I'm…" He took a breath and met my gaze. "Just, while I was still awake last night, I was thinking about some of the stuff we talked about."

My gut clenched. Oh no. Tell me he wasn't regretting it all in the light of day.

Ahmed searched my eyes. "Did you mean what you said?" He swept his tongue across his lips. "That you've…"

"That I loved you before Peyton ever bought that bottle?"

Ahmed nodded shyly.

"Yeah." I touched his face, still marveling that I could. "I've been in love with you for a long, long time."

He closed his eyes and pressed his cheek into my hand. "I can't believe I never noticed."

"You weren't supposed to."

He met my gaze, the unspoken question written on his face.

I half-shrugged. "You were with Mark. I didn't think you were happy, but it wasn't my place to sabotage your relationship or try to pull you away from him, you know?"

Ahmed swallowed. "What if I'd stayed with him? What if we'd…I don't know, gotten married or something?"

It took all I had not to shudder at the thought. Ahmed didn't need to know I'd had literal nightmares about a wedding between him and Mark.

I cupped Ahmed's face and stroked his cheekbone with my thumb, wishing like hell I could kiss him right now. Damn morning breath. "If you'd married him, then I'd still be here. You're my friend, first and foremost. I'd rather have you as a friend than not at all. It was just hard to watch you with him. Not because I was jealous—" I paused. "Okay, I *was* jealous. I can't lie. But that isn't why it was hard to watch. I just hated seeing you so unhappy."

He watched me for a moment. Then he smiled and touched my face. "You've always been an amazing friend. I'm lucky as hell to have you as a boyfriend, too."

The knot in my chest unwound and I couldn't resist—I leaned in to kiss his forehead. "I think I'm the lucky one here."

Ahmed shrugged. "Eh, we're both happy. That's the important thing, right?"

"It is." And my God, was I committed to making sure this man was as happy as humanly possible.

He shifted a little, and winced. "Ugh. We should probably get up. We're getting too old for this."

"Pfft. Speak for yourself."

"Yeah, yeah. Shut up." He tilted his head one way, then the other, as if to loosen some tension. "As long as we're out here, the café serves a decent breakfast if you're hungry."

My stomach answered for me.

"Yeah," he said with a laugh. "Me, too." But then his brow furrowed. "Wait. Do you hear that?"

I listened. "Hear what?"

"Exactly." He pushed himself up a little. "It's so quiet."

Now that he mentioned it...

I mean, I didn't expect a carnival to be hopping this early in the morning, but the silence was...expansive. Even if everyone was asleep and everything was shut down, we were in the parking lot of a pretty sizeable carnival. There should've been some noise. Generators, maybe. Flags or banners fluttering in the gentle breeze. Something.

There was nothing, though.

Ahmed and I exchanged puzzled looks.

Then we both sat up.

And for a moment, we were as still and silent as our surroundings.

Everything was gone. The tents. The booths. The rides. There wasn't another vehicle in sight. No people. No buildings. All the signs were gone. The cones and flags used to direct traffic in the parking area were gone.

The only evidence that there had been anything here at all was the somewhat straight lines of tire tracks worn into the grass, the tamped-down dirt road everyone had used to come and go, and what I swore was the faint scent of popcorn on the air. There was just enough left to keep me from wondering if I'd imagined the whole thing—though admittedly, I did still wonder, because apart from those vague remnants, it was all just…gone.

"Uh." Ahmed turned to me. "Is this weird? Because this seems weird."

"It's weird as hell." I dug my keys out of the toolbox where I'd left them last night. "How about we get out of here before the aliens come back for us or something?"

He snorted. "Good idea."

With a little groaning and creaking, we got up out of the truck bed and hopped down onto the dirt. I wadded up the blankets and shoved them behind the seats, though I would definitely be washing them when I got home.

Then we got into the truck. We'd left our phones in here last night, and we both paused to check texts and emails.

"Oh, hey," I said. "I got a message from Lucas."

"Yeah, me too." Ahmed frowned at his screen. Then he exhaled. "Oh, thank God."

I agreed—we'd both gotten the same message, and Lucas explained that he'd finally had a breakthrough with Tina. She'd come clean, and they'd been right: she'd been hiding a serious drinking problem. Apparently she'd sobbed and apologized, begging him not to leave her, and Lucas—to the surprise of neither of us—had assured her he wasn't going anywhere. They'd get her some help, and they'd put the wedding on hold just to take some stress off her shoulders.

She thought I was calling off the engagement, Lucas had written. *But I think she gets it now. I think she's relieved.*

Glad to hear she's getting some help, I wrote back. *Let me know if there's anything I can do.*

What he said, Ahmed followed. *We've all got you. And her.*

Thanks, guys. Last night was rough, but she's better this morning. Already talking about a smaller wedding, too.

"Probably smart," Ahmed said to me as he wrote back more words of encouragement. "I know she had her heart set on a big wedding, but if it's stressing her out this much…"

"Right? Man, I hope she can get sober."

"She can." He put his phone into his pocket. "She's got Lucas and her family, and they've got all of us for support. They'll be fine."

"Let's hope." I flicked my eyes toward the stretch of grass and dirt where I swore the rides and tents had been just a few hours ago. "Guess that artist really did see something in her that the rest of us didn't."

"Makes you wonder what else he sees in people."

I shivered. That artist's insight had revealed Tina's drinking problem, my feelings for Ahmed, and his misery in his relationship. In the end, all those revelations had worked out for the better. But what *else* could he see in *other* people, and how would *those* situations play out?

I wasn't so sure I wanted to know.

Without another word, I put the truck in gear, and we both cast a few wary backward glances as I drove us out of the vacant field where the bizarre carnival had been for the past few weeks.

"That was definitely weird." Ahmed chafed his arms as I turned onto the highway. "Like, everything about it."

"It was." I reached over and put a hand on his knee. "But I'm glad we went."

He covered my hand with his. "Yeah, me too. God knows how long it would've taken for this to work out if we'd never gone. Or *if* it would've."

I didn't want to think about that.

Turning my hand over beneath his, I smiled at him. "I think it all worked out exactly the way it needed to."

"Yeah." He ran his thumb along mine. "Absolutely perfectly."

Understatement of the year.

We pulled into the café and enjoyed a leisurely breakfast, bantering all the way in between flirting and exchanging wicked grins. By the time I dropped him off at his place so we could shower and take care of our Saturday adulting, we'd already decided to meet up again this evening. Dinner. Movie. Maybe a blowjob in the Dick's parking lot.

Whatever we did, I had no doubt it would be amazing.

And even though that weird little carnival kind of creeped me out, I couldn't lie:

I hoped it came back this way next summer.

ABOUT THE AUTHOR

L.A. Witt is a romance and suspense author who has at last given up the exciting nomadic lifestyle of the military spouse (read: her husband finally retired). She now resides in Pittsburgh, where the potholes are determined to eat her car and her cats are endlessly taunted by a disrespectful squirrel named Moose. In her spare time, she can be found painting in her art room or destroying her voice at a Pittsburgh Penguins game.

Website: http://www.gallagherwitt.com
Twitter: https://twitter.com/GallagherWitt
Instagram: https://www.instagram.com/gallagherwitt/
Facebook Group: https://www.facebook.com/groups/1633167680026803

CARNIVAL OF MYSTERIES

Welcome, Traveler! Join us for a series of M/M fantasies by a talented group of both new and established authors. Whether you enjoy mystery, action, danger, or just sweet romance, there is something for everyone at the Carnival of Mysteries!

Kim Fielding * L. A. Witt * Kaje Harper

Megan Derr * Ander C. Lark * E. J. Russell

Morgan Brice * Sarah Ellis * Kayleigh Sky

Nicole Dennis * Elizabeth Silver * Ro Merrill

T. A. Moore * Z. A. Maxfield * Ki Brightly

Rachel Langella